# Winding up the Serpent

# Serpent

## Priscilla Masters

This edition published in Great Britain in 1997 by
Allison & Busby Ltd
114 New Cavendish Street
London W1M 7FD

First published in Great Britain by
Macmillan in 1995

A catalogue record for this book is available from the
British Library

ISBN 0 74900 371 5

Printed and bound in Great Britain by
Mackays of Chatham Plc
Chatham, Kent

0749  003  715  3520

'And the Lord said unto Moses, Make thee a fiery serpent, and set it upon a pole: and it shall come to pass, that everyone that is bitten, when he looketh upon it, shall live.'

(*Numbers*, ch. 21 v. 13)

This 'snake on a stick' is the emblem of the British Medical Association.

To my long-suffering family,
and to Chief Superintendent Philip Rushton
for questions answered meticulously

# Chapter 1

It was the dog, Ben, who first knew something was wrong. When the alarm clock clicked on at 6.55 he opened one brown eye and waited. Nothing happened. He dropped a huge paw over the side of his basket and sat up on his haunches, waiting for the familiar sounds ... rustling of bedclothes, soft foot on the floor, steps to the bathroom. He opened the other eye.

In the bedroom the clock radio chattered brightly. The dog gave a low growl and padded to the foot of the stairs, his tail down.

Dogs are supposed to be more sensitive to atmosphere than humans. Apparently civilization has bred out human instinct for danger. So it was fitting that it should be the dog who first knew something was wrong. Because he was a dog he did not know what, but he bounded up the stairs, across the landing, and pushed the bedroom door further open with his nose, peering round cautiously. Then he crossed the room in two great strides and waited expectantly by the bed. His mistress did not wake.

He gave a quiet whine and took up a patient watching post at the foot of the bed, like a sphinx, with his head between his paws.

Number 17 Silk Street was the house next door. At eight o'clock Evelyn Shiers took up her post, peeped through the yellow curtains, hiding at the side of the window. She didn't want Marilyn to see her watching. But neither did she want Ben to enter her garden. He frightened the cats

1

and left torpedoes on what was left of the lawn and flower-beds. He frightened her, too. Already she could feel her mouth dry in dread of the confrontation, and the muscles at the back of her neck tightened, threatening yet another miserable migraine. She mounted guard, pleating and unpleating the fingermarked material, her eyes trained on the flower-bed, blinking quickly in case she missed the quick, grey movement of the dog.

This morning Ben did not appear.

Back at number 19 the wind was blowing the bedroom curtain, whipping the lace mats on the dressing table to a pink froth. Ben wagged his tail tentatively now, certain his mistress would soon move, swing her legs over the side of the bed, bend and touch him, pad to the bathroom then fill his bowls with food and water.

He watched the figure on the bed with extra attention; soon she must move. The breeze lifted the curtain again but there was no echoing movement from the bed and his tail gradually stopped thumping on the carpet. Ben whimpered, and glanced around the room.

He sniffed. The scent was the same, sweet and definitely her. He eyed the Spanish flamenco doll that stood in the corner and gave a low, threatening growl. He had once been punished for daring to lick it. He sniffed again. Even now it smelt alien. His nostrils twitched. He caught the faint odour of something long ago, something pleasant, something half remembered. He looked up at the still figure on the bed and gave a low, experimental bark. This always provoked response. This morning there was none.

Nobody missed her at the surgery. The doctor was busy, talking to his first patient. He let down the sphygmomanometer cuff with a hiss and unhooked the stethoscope from around his ears. 'Your blood pressure's fine today, Mary.' His eyes crinkled as he smiled and seeing this she smiled too.

'Thank you, Doctor.'

'I want you to carry on with the treatment. Just two tablets a day. One in the morning and one at night.' It was a formality and forestalled her questions. There was no time. Already he was scribbling in her notes, his attention starting to move from this patient to the next.

Mary stood up and left the room and the doctor pressed the buzzer for his second patient.

She was always conscious of an unnatural silence as she walked towards the door bearing her name, Detective Inspector Piercy. There should have been sounds – drawers opening and closing, typewriter keys clicking, computers whirring, telephones ringing. But the silence always seemed to conspire against her so she ran the gauntlet, avoided curious gazes, muttered, 'Good morning,' vaguely, and reached the room.

Once inside she flicked on the light, turned off the heating and threw open the window. The mist had cleared and the sun shone on an eggshell-blue sky. Spring was here, the time of new beginnings. She had her longed-for promotion, why did she feel depressed?

A sudden hot surge of frustration welled up inside her. It was all so unfair. She'd been awarded the position because she was good – better than those two who sat at their desks penning clumsy reports riddled with spelling mistakes. But all they could see was that she was a woman.

It had been she who had finally put the evidence together that had pinned the Whalleys behind prison bars. They had had their chance and failed. They'd all known – for eight, nine years – that one family had, between them, burgled virtually every house in the whole of this tiny moorland town. But the apathy of the local force had meant they had never bothered to work out a successful way to gather the evidence necessary to convict them. Six times they had brought weak, watery cases in front of the Crown Prosecution Service and six times the case had been thrown out.

Insufficient evidence. It just wasn't worth the cost to

bring the whole case to court and it had been the morale of the local force that had suffered – that and the homes of the people of this small, crime-infested town. It had taken her just three weeks' surveillance, a video camera, a couple of well-timed warrants and a notable lack of flashing blue lights and the drama they all loved so much.

'Bang the bloody light off, Sergeant,' she had snapped. 'Don't bloody well announce we're coming. This isn't for the benefit of the BBC.' It had been the tight sarcasm the two other officers had resented and not forgotten, the searing scorn for their traditional police methods and a dislike for the woman who had so publicly challenged them and found them inadequate.

'Surprise them,' she had said smoothly, 'and perhaps for once we'll actually get a conviction and tuck this little bunch up for a few nights' safe and sound sleep at Her Majesty's five-star instead of having them leering at us as they leave our little police station.'

And she'd got them. The whole family, Ma as well, and it gave her great pleasure every time she drove out on the Buxton road and saw the For Sale sign at the bottom of the half-mile dirt track. This scruffy, isolated farmhouse had been home to the family responsible for more than half the crimes committed in this small town sealed in by high, hostile moorland.

She had been rewarded, too. Detective Sergeant Piercy had become Detective Inspector Piercy. But the promotion had sown the seeds of resentment in her junior colleagues. And new team members were quickly warned.

'Keep away from Inspector Piercy, the Ice Maiden, the Snow Queen . . .' She knew what they called her, and what they said. '. . . Thinks she's too clever, too good for the rest of us. Has some sort of illusion she's one of these clever dicks.' (Coarse laughter.) 'Thinks she's a cross between Sherlock Holmes and Juliet Bravo. She's a cold bitch, that one.'

She could hear the words with all their hostility and

prejudice every time she saw any of them, heads together, talking quietly and glancing at her. Thank God for her own room. To have to sit out there all day and see them every time she looked up would have been intolerable.

Joanna Piercy turned away from the window and rubbed her hands down the sides of her straight black skirt. 'Bugger them,' she said loudly. 'Bugger them.' Then, 'Bugger them,' again.

She strode to the door and threw it open. 'Anything either of you two want to report?' she asked sharply, as though the very question was a fresh challenge. It was the only way to survive here – to keep her anger fresh and her faculties sharp by reminding them she was their superior officer, like it or not. And they didn't.

The two men looked up at her briefly, shook their heads and looked back at the notes in front of them.

'Couple of stolen mountain bikes,' the younger, fair-haired policeman mumbled. The officer with the black hair scowled.

'Mike?' she asked sweetly.

He shook his head. 'Nothing,' he grunted.

She banged the door behind her.

Ben was getting hungry. He crawled towards the bed, whining, and put one paw up. The claw snagged the lace bedspread. The hair on the back of his neck bristled and he pulled. The lace tore. His claw was free. But the action brought a belt sliding to the floor, weighted by a silver buckle. It landed with a soft, metallic thud. Ben walked around the belt, sniffing it suspiciously. It, at least, was familiar. Emboldened, he put his paw up again and this time it touched a leg. Again his claw caught. He tugged and tore a hole. A white ladder ran up the black stocking until it reached the dark band at the top. Ben's dog-brown eyes watched, fascinated, then he gave a fearful yowl and bounded downstairs towards the ringing tele-phone in the hall.

*

At the doctor's surgery the two receptionists were in a quandary. A patient had come to the window and demanded to know why Sister Smith had not rung her buzzer for him. He was half an hour late for his next appointment. What was going on?

Maureen had knocked on the nurse's door and realized the room was empty. They had rung her home and got no reply. Should they tell the doctor? They eyed the clock uneasily as the minutes ticked away. Two of the patients walked out, muttering they could wait no longer.

At half past nine the red-headed receptionist knocked on the doctor's surgery door.

He looked up irritably. 'Yes, Sally?' He hated interruptions.

'I'm sorry to barge in, Doctor,' she said. 'Sister Smith hasn't come in.'

Jonah Wilson frowned. 'Is she having a day off?'

The receptionist shook her head. 'She's got eleven patients booked in this morning, Doctor, and more this afternoon.'

Jonah frowned and sighed. 'Well, ring her,' he said. 'There isn't much point in bothering me. I've got enough to do.' He turned back to the patient and the pile of notes.

Sally fiddled with the loose button on the sleeve of her blouse. Before the end of the morning she would pull it right off. 'I did ring,' she said. 'There was no answer.'

Jonah sighed again and tugged a pile of letters out of the Lloyd George envelope. 'Then she's probably on her way in,' he said.

Sally could be persistent. 'I rang her half an hour ago.' Her eyes met his. 'It would only take her ten minutes at the most to get from her house to here. Besides, she's not usually late. Marilyn's reliable.'

Jonah shrugged his shoulders. 'Keep trying her,' he said. 'I expect she's overslept or had a flat tyre. There's been a muddle. She'll turn up.'

'She would have rung,' the receptionist insisted.

He looked up briefly. 'The line's always engaged,' he

said, irritably. 'You can never get through in the mornings.'

Sally still looked dissatisfied but she could think of no other avenue to pursue.

The doctor sighed, shrugged his shoulders and shifted his attention away from the problem of the missing nurse and back to his patient.

Sally left the room.

# Chapter 2

Ben had been unnerved by the sight of the white ladder running up the leg, but curiosity brought him back to the bedroom. His head turned as he watched the breeze lift first the curtain then touch his mistress's hair, blowing it across her face. He walked slowly around the bed until he sniffed out a single glass, its contents spilt. He licked the sticky stain then looked up guiltily. This was another smacking offence. His mistress smacked hard. He put his head on one side, then sprang up and put his two front paws on the bed. This was not allowed either, but Ben was beginning to lose his fear of his mistress. He bent over her and stared at the still figure. He sniffed, then licked her mouth and barked loudly.

Joanna settled down to some paperwork. The town had a problem. In fact it had two pressing problems. The first – and the one that captured the headlines in the local paper – was the persistent theft of Royal Doulton figures. Each week – Joanna leafed through the sheafs of burglary claims – between thirty and forty Doulton figures were stolen from local houses. And the good citizens were getting very tired of the loss of the pretty china dancing ladies. The thieves were clever. They had plenty of knowledge and they were audacious, too. She picked up one of the claim forms. They had left behind any pieces that were chipped. She picked up another of the insurance forms. On another occasion they had stolen the genuine article and left the 'seconds' or rejects, cheap prizes brought home like trophies by the pottery workers. Twice the thieves had left copies of Royal Doulton figures standing on the mantelpieces while they lifted the real McCoy. And it was this audacity that was infuriating the editorial department of the local rag, who had penned some very choice headlines. Because, although close on two thousand figurines had been stolen in the last two years, not one single piece of china had ever been recovered. And Joanna knew that her reply – to use fluorescent pen to mark the post code on the underside of the figurines – just wasn't good enough. They needed a lead to get to the stolen pieces to inspect them and *find* the post code. Worst of all, Joanna knew they had no clues either to who was committing the crimes or to how they were processing the stolen figures. To her knowledge not one of them had so far come up for sale. The best they could hope for was a 'mole', someone to give them the vital hint. She sighed.

If the local population was getting fed up, she was frankly worried. The theft of china dancing ladies was a crime. But the recent supplying of Ecstasy to one of the local primary schools frightened her. An Ecstasy tablet sent for analysis had uncovered not only amphetamine but tiny doses of crack cocaine. She knew the results of the infiltration of the drug dealers, and she knew the impact they could have on this small town. The pushers were always searching to widen their net – more customers meant more money. Young customers meant money for life – as long or short as the life might be. And the dealers didn't care whether the kids lived or died – they could always get more. It was the mums and dads, the brothers and sisters and friends who cared – sometimes.

The pushers worried her. They were callous and amoral and left a trail of devastation in their wake. It was up to the police to try to sort out the muddle.

She sat staring into space.

The drugs were pouring in. And not one of her

informers seemed to have the slightest idea how a small town had such an endless and unlimited supply, or how to stem the flow.

By eleven o'clock Jonah Wilson was at the undertaker's, staring down at a pale, flabby body.

He glanced across at his friend. 'I'll miss the old bugger.'

Paul Haddon grinned at Jonah, raising his hooded, dark eyes. 'It's a miracle he lived as long as he did, the way he abused his body.' Haddon laughed. 'The number of times I've almost knocked him down with my hearse. Staggering into the road, drunk.'

Jonah frowned, then pressed the bell of his stethoscope on to the man's chest. He nodded. 'As a door nail,' he said. 'Cremation?'

Haddon nodded.

Jonah looked down. 'Heart,' he said. 'The coroner's happy. No need for a post-mortem. I'd been expecting it for years. No need to upset the family more than we have to.' He looked up. 'Paul . . .?'

The undertaker had been standing still, staring down at the dead man. He started at the sound of his name, shook. 'Sorry, Jonah,' he said. 'Sorry . . . miles away.'

Jonah put a hand on his friend's arm. 'No regrets, Paul?'

'No,' said the undertaker, biting his lip. 'Not really.'

Jonah turned away from the body to wash his hands at the sink. 'By the way,' he said, 'Smithy didn't turn up for work this morning.'

Haddon stared at him. 'Didn't she?'

Jonah shook his head.

'Did you try ringing?'

'The girls did.'

'And?'

'No reply. No one in.'

'So where was she?'

The men looked at one another.

Paul spoke first. 'What about Ben?'

Jonah shook his head. He closed his Gladstone bag then stood up. 'Perhaps I should go round,' he said tentatively. 'See if she's all right.'

His friend put a restraining hand on his arm. 'I wouldn't if I were you, Jonah,' he said. 'I'd leave her well alone. Let someone else find her.'

Jonah looked dubious. 'But I'm her employer,' he said. 'She could be hurt. She could be lying there, in pain . . . fallen or something. Who else will go?'

'Someone will.' Paul spoke grimly. 'And if no one does, all the better.'

'Paul.' Jonah shook his friend's hand off his arm.

'I don't know how you can care at all about her,' Paul said. 'I don't have your nature, Jonah. I can't forgive her.' He stared across the room. 'She's ruined more lives . . . caused more unhappiness . . .' He looked at his friend then. 'I hate her,' he said. 'I hate her.' He shook his head. 'I wouldn't go round if I were you. Leave it alone.'

His dark eyes stared into the doctor's face and as he spoke he nodded meaningfully, gripping the doctor's arm now. 'Leave it alone,' he said again. 'Don't you get involved.'

Jonah looked confused and embarrassed. 'What if—' he started urgently.

'Forget "what if"! Forget it, Jonah.'

The doctor sighed. His shoulders drooped. 'Something might have happened to her.'

'We can all live in hope,' said the undertaker darkly.

Jonah picked up his bag. 'I'm going, Paul,' he said.

Haddon gripped his arm again. 'I mean it, Jonah,' he said urgently. 'Promise me you won't go.'

Jonah frowned. 'I . . .'

'Promise.'

'I promise.'

Ben was desperate to be let out. Desperate and frightened, too. He gave a whine then a series of loud barks.

11

In the bedroom nothing stirred. The breeze had dropped. Outside it began to rain. Droplets splattered on the windowsill. Ben barked again, watched the bed. Nothing moved.

He darted downstairs, sniffed behind the sofa. Then he squatted uneasily. If she found it she would beat him. He finished and guiltily ran back upstairs.

If she found it.

He put two paws on the bed, licked the cold hand.

By eleven o'clock Evelyn Shiers had finished at the market. She walked into the kitchen and dumped her shopping bag on the table. Strange, she thought, as she caught sight of the red car standing in her neighbour's drive. Was she on holiday this week? Before she switched on the radio she stood still for a minute listening, her ear cocked like an animal's for sounds from next door. Silence. Then she heard Ben whining and that made no sense. Marilyn was at home. Her car was in the drive. Why should the dog whine? She frowned as her thoughts progressed slowly towards conclusion. 'Don't be silly,' she muttered. 'She's on holiday. She's in the house – or walking in the town.'

So why, her small, inner voice said, didn't she take the dog with her, or put him in the pen outside? Why was he whining? And there was no answer to that.

'Try her again,' Sally urged, pushing Maureen towards the telephone. 'The doctor won't see all her evening patients as well. She'll have to come in, hangover or no hangover.'

Maureen looked at her. 'Have you ever known Sister Smith to have a hangover?'

Sally pressed the number quickly. She had dialled it so many times this morning she knew it by heart. 'She must have a hangover. She was all right yesterday and she's never ill. And she hasn't rung...' Her voice trailed into nothing and she replaced the receiver.

Jonah left the undertaker's with a sudden sense of freedom. Spring was in the air. The weather was bright and clean and the journey across the moors to the small isolated village of Flash fitted in with the dream he had always had of English country general practice. If only Pamella could have been with him it would have been perfect. But she would never come now and this was his sadness, because his dream had always been to share this and not to be alone. He glanced at his bag which now occupied her seat and he tried to concentrate on the patient he was about to see, on one of his regular home visits, an old man who had smoked all his life and was now dependent on cylinders of oxygen to give him breath. It wouldn't be long before he paid the ultimate price for a packet of the cigarettes he had loved.

The wife was a stringy old bird of seventy-five or thereabouts and she looked after him hand and foot, kept him out of hospital and still washed the sheets by hand, with water drawn from a well. One day Flash would be fed piped water and for a few years families would value it as a luxury. Until then it would have to survive on wells and springs.

It was as Jonah groped in his bag to check for a syringe that the second thing went wrong that morning. He found to his annoyance that he had run out of fine insulin needles. He rummaged around in the bottom of the bag with one hand, keeping his eyes on the road. He frowned. He could have sworn he had a couple left. He must have used them all. Damn. But at least this distracted him from his sense of loss.

Evelyn fidgeted all morning, unable to settle to her usual round of duster flicking, vacuum cleaning and spraying indiscriminately with scented polish. She was drawn too frequently towards the window to make an efficient job

13

of the cleaning and she kept peeping out through the curtains for a sign of Marilyn's pudgy figure, listening all the time for the click-clack of Marilyn's stilettos. She heard nothing but the dog's crescendo of yowls. Eventually she stopped altogether, her hand on her duster poised in front of her. She had never heard Ben whine like this. He was generally a quiet dog, well used to his life chained up outside in a pen, a guard dog who kept the house safe by day when the nurse was out working. And in the night the dog kept guard by sleeping at the foot of the stairs in a huge basket. This noisy behaviour was unusual – so strange it made her feel sick and uneasy.

She watched the house for signs of movement, concentrating on the brightly painted pink front door with its brass knocker, its huge brass hinges and letterbox. She stared at the door, willing it to open, hardly caring now that Marilyn might see her. In fact she would be relieved to see her, might even wave. But the door remained firmly shut. She glanced at the windows. The downstairs curtains were drawn. The red Astra sat motionless in the drive.

And still there was no sign of movement and no sound except the dog's anguished howls punctuated by frenzied, maddened yapping.

All morning she thought of walking up the drive, knocking on the door and shouting, asking whether something was the matter, but she was put off by the dog. Evelyn had always been a little frightened by Ben. And there was that incident about a year ago . . .

. . . She had been idly glancing out of the kitchen window – not spying – but she had seen a van pull up abruptly at the foot of the drive. A man had jumped out, slammed the door, run up the drive and hammered on the front door, shouting, swearing obscenities.

Evelyn's heart fluttered at the memory.

Marilyn's dumpy figure had appeared in the doorway, hands on hips. She had been wearing a satin thing, fallen

14

open to reveal plump breasts. She had laughed at the man, shouted back, sworn to match his expletives. She had stepped towards him and the satin thing had slipped off her shoulders so that almost the full breast was exposed, pink crescent of nipple showing. She'd wagged her finger in the man's face, cavernous red mouth wide open. They had both shouted and then Marilyn's voice had dropped suddenly and the man seemed subdued. Then Marilyn had glanced across and seen her watching.

Both had turned on her with a torrent of foul, ugly language and Evelyn had dropped to the floor, shaking and frightened. She heard Marilyn shouting, threatening to set the dog on her. She had been frightened of Marilyn Smith ever since . . .

So instead of approaching the house she did other things to absorb her attention, plumping up cushions, wiping the front doorstep, attending to a cupboard that needed sorting out. But when men's sweaters, shirts, ties, socks tumbled out in a woollen jumble she shuddered, picked them up, stuffed them back in the cupboard again and slammed the door shut.

She muttered to herself and polished windows, dusted shelves, washed the kitchen floor. But she left the radio switched off, and every few minutes she stood by the kitchen window and peered over the low wall at the house and listened to the noisy barks.

It was at lunchtime that she knew something was definitely wrong.

Marilyn would not have left the dog alone inside the house for so long. He would have wrecked it. Marilyn was in there too. Evelyn stared at the house with mounting fear and she wrung her hands because she didn't know what to do. 'Oh, help,' she said. 'Please – somebody must help me.'

Ben was terrified now. He whined and slunk across the bedroom floor, tail down. He watched the still figure on

15

the bed and knew she would find the mess downstairs.
Then she would beat him.

He growled and whined, then ran downstairs into the
kitchen. Some drops from the dripping tap slaked his
thirst. He licked some meat from a plate on the side.
Then he bounded upstairs again ...

When two o'clock struck and there was still no sign of
movement and the only sounds were the yelps of the dog,
Evelyn telephoned the surgery and asked for Sister
Smith.

If only Marilyn would pick up the phone at the other
end. But when her call was answered she said only, 'Sister
Smith.' Then she panicked and threw the receiver down
on to its cradle.

Jonah watched his old patient gasping for breath. With a
tinge of pity he touched the old man's hand.

'Jack,' he said, 'you're very bad today. You need the
hospital. I can't keep you alive here.' He spoke slowly
and clearly in short sentences.

The old man understood. He closed his eyes and
answered in a dry, rasping voice. 'If I'm too bad for home,
Doctor, I'm too bad to live. No hospital for me. I don't
want a couple of days – maybe months – bought at that
price.'

The pauses between words grew longer and on the last
word he closed his eyes. Neither of the two people
watching would have been surprised if he had not
spoken again.

His wife touched Jonah's arm. 'Let 'im stay here,
Doctor. If 'is time has come so be it.' Her face was set
and hard, unsmiling, her leathered complexion timeless,
strong and unyielding. The moors toughened their
women.

Jonah nodded. 'So be it.'

The old man struggled to open his eyes. 'Yes, Doctor.
She's right.' He snapped the oxygen mask back over his

16

nose and mouth. It steamed up with his breath and the wrinkled eyelids closed again wearily. His face was gaunt and grey with the struggle.

'I can give you an injection,' Jonah said. 'It'll help the breathing.' He looked again at the old man. 'Are you sure you wouldn't like a bed in the hospital – just to give your wife a break?'

The old man clawed the doctor's hand and he shook his head. 'No,' he said. 'I'll die if I go in there.'

Jonah bit back the obvious answer. He took from his bag a syringe and an ampoule of Aminophylline. Carefully he put a tourniquet on the skinny arm, selected a prominent blue rope vein and drove the drug in. The old man's eyes closed.

By three in the afternoon the dog's obvious distress was becoming more than Evelyn could bear. She stood with her cup of tea by the kitchen window, listening to the yowling.

She was suddenly so sure that Marilyn would not appear in the doorway and climb into the car as she had watched her do a thousand times that Evelyn did an unbelievable thing. She took a deep breath, unlocked the front door, marched through the pink lions rampant on Marilyn's gatepost, walked up to the front door, raised the letterbox and dropped it again, pressed the doorbell and shouted Marilyn's name. Her voice bounced around the walls.

But the dog bounded down the stairs with a fierce growl and it terrified her so she ran back to the house and rang the surgery again.

'Please,' she spoke into the phone, 'please, is Marilyn Smith there? Something is wrong with her dog.' The words tumbled out and she replaced the receiver without giving the other end a chance to speak.

In the surgery Maureen, who had taken the call, stood and stared at the telephone, blinking behind owlish

17

glasses. She felt cold and uneasy. Dead hands stole up her back. 'It was that person again,' she said, 'asking for Sister Smith.'

'Ring the police,' Sally said decisively. 'Ring them now.' And when her colleague didn't move she grabbed the phone. 'Ring the bloody police.'

# Chapter 3

The slick white car with its fluorescent pink strip had been cruising near the market square, its occupants checking that inconsiderately parked cars were not blocking the narrow road and keeping an eye on a gang of youths clustered outside the video shop, when it took the call. It switched on its flashing blue light and sped up the High Street, turned right into Silk Street and arrived minutes later. The two uniformed policemen crunched up the gravel drive and in passing tried the door of the parked car. It was locked. They knocked at the front door and were rewarded by Ben's frantic barks.

They looked at one another uncertainly. 'I don't fancy meeting him face to face,' said one of them.

They shouted through the letterbox, feeling slightly foolish. 'Hello! Anyone at home? Are you there, Miss Smith? He-ll-o! Hello, Miss Smith. Mar-i-lun!'

Only the dog responded and they quickly dropped the flap. They walked around the back of the house, trying windows while the dog followed them from room to room, alternating mad barks with hostile growls. They watched him through the window, then went back to the car and sent a message over the radio.

'No one around, dog going mad. No sign of a break-in. Have to get in but need help with the dog.'

'Message received ... Over.'

Detective Sergeant Mike Korpanski replaced the receiver, scribbling down the details in his notebook.

He knew instinctively this was no hoax. They wouldn't break in then meet her returning from a night away or a shopping spree. That much they knew from the dog's behaviour, but out of habit Mike tried Marilyn Smith's number himself. As he had expected, no one picked up the phone. He replaced the set.

He ran over the facts quickly in his mind . . . A single woman, fortyish, lived alone, in good health. Unexpectedly she had failed to turn up at work. She had not answered the phone and a couple of strange telephone calls had been made to the surgery, asking for her then hanging up without leaving a name. Car in the drive, locked. No obvious sign of a break-in, according to the uniformed lads. Dog whining.

And this was the alarm call. According to the surgery she was devoted to the dog; they were inseparable. She never left him except when she went to work and then the dog was safely put in a pen outside. DS Korpanski glanced at the closed door and grimaced. He supposed he'd have to tell her.

Mike, as he liked to be called, was more than six feet tall, dark-eyed with black hair bottle-brush short, and a thick bull neck. His father had been a loyal Pole, tempted to fight for the British, then seduced to stay by a local woman. Mike was their only, adored son. Devoted to body building, his shape revealed the hours he spent every week at the gym, pumping iron. With bulging biceps, a straight, strong back and heavy hamstrings, he was a popular member of the force, a supervisory officer for the juniors to emulate. And cheerful, too, with a ready grin and a good nature – except when he was either embarrassed or angry or both, as he was now. He knocked on DI Piercy's door and waited, despising himself for having to stand outside until her whim called him in.

He planted himself legs apart in front of her desk, so close he could almost have touched the thick dark hair that just touched the crisp white blouse. Her hands rolled a pen between her slim fingers as she listened to what he had to say, her head tilted upwards, intelligent blue eyes fixing on his as she concentrated. And the furrow between her eyebrows, which never quite left her face even when she laughed, deepened as she frowned. It took him seconds to fill her in and he watched her eyes shine at the challenge and knew that however wide the gulf was between them – and it was wide – they shared at least one thing – love of the work.

As soon as he had finished she cleared her throat and fired a few abrupt questions.

'Who was it who rang the surgery?'

'We don't know.'

'When was she last seen?'

'Yesterday, about five, when she left work.'

Without saying another word she stood up, unhooked her jacket from the back of the chair and slipped it on over the white blouse.

'Lead on,' she said smartly. 'Lead on, Sergeant.'

'Yes, madam.' The tight sarcasm made his voice sound tired and disillusioned. He felt suddenly bitter as she moved towards the door, unmistakably feminine, a waft of light, clean perfume that touched his nostrils emphasizing the fact.

Joanna tightened her mouth at his tone and her frank smile evaporated.

'Did you say there was a dog?' she asked sharply.

He nodded. 'Yes, a German Shepherd and the neighbour said it's trained as a guard dog. Apparently it acts like a bodyguard to the woman.'

'Very sensible,' she said approvingly, 'for a single woman, living alone.' She met Mike's eyes unflinchingly. 'Perhaps I should invest in one, Sergeant.'

He nodded. 'Perhaps you should.' He stood awkwardly, miserably uncertain, finding his position too uncomfortable until she spoke decisively.

21

'So ring the vet.'

Mike flushed. 'Right, ma'am.'

The vet turned up in an old mud-splattered green Landrover.

Joanna wrinkled her nose. 'Have you driven through a cowshed to get here?'

The vet laughed, taking no offence. 'Scent of the country, Inspector,' he said. 'If you want to work in an area that stinks of CFCs and "Country Meadow" from Sainsbury's you'd better return to the city. I happen to prefer the real thing.' He grinned at her and held out his hand. 'Inspector Piercy, I presume. I'm Roderick Beeston.'

She found it difficult to resent his good-natured, blunt manner. Instead she smiled. 'I think we have a difficult dog,' she said.

The vet's eyes narrowed. 'Really?'

There was a good-humoured look on his face but she knew his opinion was that it was never the dog who was difficult. She hurried Mike into the squad car and the vet followed in the Landrover.

She glanced back at him a couple of times during the journey and saw him grinning at her over the wheel, one hand casually waving while the other loosely steered the car. Once he gave a vigorous thumbs-up sign and mouthed some words. She could not guess what. His window was wide open as he drew parallel to them at the traffic lights.

'I know Ben,' he shouted, 'guards his mistress well. He'd have you for breakfast and still want his sausages.'

She blushed and gave a tight smile and they started up as the lights changed, turned right then left and left again into Silk Street. Mike pulled up outside number 19 behind the first squad car.

'This looks like the house.'

She raised her eyebrows at the pair of pink lions that sat on the gateposts and wondered what sort of woman lived here and what they would find inside. Then she looked up at the detached, red-brick house with its UPVC double glazing, fancy Austrian blinds festooning the windows.

She followed the green oilskin and wellies of the vet and the heavy footsteps of DS Korpanski, passing the new red Vauxhall Astra in the drive.

'She did well for a nurse,' she remarked. 'Unless there's been a rich husband in the past.'

The vet scratched his grizzled beard. 'That sounds a remarkably sexist statement,' he said, 'coming from Leek's first female police inspector.'

Joanna flushed again and turned to Mike. 'She wasn't married?'

'Not as far as I know.'

At the top of the drive they met the two uniformed police who looked slightly sheepish and apologetic.

'We would have gone in,' one said, 'if it hadn't been for the dog.'

Joanna stood for a moment. 'It's OK,' she said absently. 'Probably just as well anyway if there is anything to find – the fewer intrusions the better.' She frowned and looked at them. 'Any broken windows – forced doors?'

'No.' They shook their heads. 'Nothing.'

She thought for a moment. 'This place wasn't bought out of a nurse's salary.'

'Or a policeman's,' Mike grunted. 'Even an inspector's.'

She heard the hostility in his tone. 'So is that it, Mike?' she said softly. 'Money. And I was thinking it was purely sex.'

'I've a family,' he said. 'That needs money.'

She bit back all the retorts. 'Let's get on with the job, for God's sake, Mike. Tuck the whole bloody package away – resentment, bitterness. There isn't any room for it. Let's just get on with the job. Besides,' she grinned, 'an inspector's salary isn't that bloody brilliant. It isn't the gateway to the millionaires' club, you know. Now, shall we get on with the job?'

Mike's black eyes seemed to boil with anger but he said nothing.

Joanna banged on the front door. 'Miss Smith . . . Miss Smith! Are you in there?'

She hesitated for a moment then tried again, shouting through the letterbox. 'Hello – is anyone at home?'

For answer they heard a deep growl followed by frenzied barking, and she drew back as the dog's black muzzle pushed against the letterbox. She looked at the vet. 'Over to you.'

Roderick Beeston nodded and he pulled a canister out of his pocket. 'I'd better give him a puffer,' he said, 'before you bang much more on that door. It's going to send him mad and I know Ben. He's a big, bad dog.'

He winked at Mike, and Joanna could feel the empathy between the two men which seemed to extend to the uniformed officers standing behind them and which excluded her.

'Well, get on with it, please,' she said crisply. 'Something's wrong and the sooner we get inside that house the better. The woman might be ill.'

The vet took a canister from the back of the Landrover and a pair of thick leather gauntlets. Then he propped open the letterbox while the four police watched him. He gave a few short puffs to the excited dog and the barking softened then stopped and they heard a thud as the heavy dog hit the floor. The vet looked pleased. 'General anaesthetic,' he said. 'Lasts an hour.' He stuffed the canister back into his pocket. 'Haven't used it before,' he said. 'New on the market. Good stuff.'

'Very interesting.' Joanna tried to ignore Mike's amused face. 'Just the thing for a burglar faced with an aggressive dog.'

The vet looked at her. 'It's on the market to reduce the number of dog bites to vets,' he said. 'They can be a big problem and if, God forbid, rabies ever creeps along the Chunnel into Britain dog bites would be potentially lethal.' He frowned at her. 'Even the police might be glad of a whiff of this stuff aimed in the right direction then.

It isn't specifically targeted against the police force and for the house burglar. Don't be paranoid, Inspector,' he mocked. 'There are plenty of good things on the market that can be put to bad use. Look at glue.'

Joanna ignored the comment and the irritation that pricked her. Instead she spoke to the two uniformed officers. 'Well, what are you waiting for? We'd better break in.'

It wasn't difficult. Marilyn Smith had relied on the dog for security, and a quick tap on the glass in the door, followed by a loop of an arm through to open the Yale and they were inside, leaving the vet to care for the prostrate animal.

Inside, the house was a riot of colour: florid petunia wallpaper in the hall, violent magenta paintwork and vividly patterned carpets. They stepped into their first room.

It took less than three minutes for them to find the source of the smell. Mike stepped in the heap that Ben had deposited in desperation behind the chintz-covered sofa in the sitting room.

Leaving the three policemen downstairs, Joanna walked up the short staircase towards the threat of the first floor. She drew a blank in the bathroom: dropped clothes scattered on the floor and an oily tide-mark in the bath. There was a faint scent of musk as though the occupant had had an exotic douse a few hours before. She found it a disturbing presence.

The first bedroom was small, neat and yellow and it appeared unused; the second was a turquoise room set out specially for visitors.

It was in the third bedroom that she found the missing nurse. Again the room was brightly decorated. The curtains were drawn but gusts of wind billowed them aside so the light alternated between dappled sunshine and the rather dingy pink blush shed by two shaded lamps. The effect was seedy, artificial. But it was one of movement. Not so the woman lying on the bed.

Joanna stared at her, appalled by the theatrical,

brothel-like backdrop of the room with its main figure, the whore, lying on the bed. She had expected to find something different in the nurse's house. Not this.

'Oh, God,' she said softly. 'Oh, God.'

Marilyn Smith was lying spreadeagled across the bed, a plump figure bursting out of a tight, black, boned corset. She wore suspenders, black stockings with a wide ladder running the whole length, from the swell of her plump bulging thigh to her stocky calf, which ended in high-heeled, courtesan's shoes. She wore thick, greasy make-up – plenty of it – and her red, lipsticked mouth dropped open. Her eyes were not quite closed and peered glassily from beneath violet-smeared lids, rimmed with heavy black lines.

Joanna moved towards the bed and took in other details – the pads of white flesh that bulged between the tops of the stockings and the lace-covered crotch, sprouting dark pubic hair – and her feelings wavered between revulsion and swamping pity for the dead woman. But all the time she was noting the details she would eventually relate to the coroner. Tuck away any dangerous and blushing comparisons, Inspector, she thought. This is a victim on the bed; not you.

There is no confusing death. No one looking over a dead person could wonder whether they still lived. Because there is a colour of death – a blotched paleness, lividity of the lower limbs where the blood has drained. The eyes are those of a dead fish and the skin sags. There is a draining too of personality and then there is a chill. Because a dead person gives out no warmth. Joanna drew in a deep breath to push away nausea. She had never quite got used to the presence of the Grim Reaper, especially when presented in such an obscene pose.

She stared with a mounting, sick feeling at what could only be described as Marilyn's seduction garments, black lace, suspenders, legs dropped apart displaying to the full a scarlet and black G-string, breasts forced prominent by firm boning of a black basque, arms stretched upwards in an abandoned pose revealing recently shaved underarms. Joanna peered closer and noted specks of blood from the shaving, mingled with beads of cold sweat. The curtains blew open suddenly and Marilyn Smith lay exposed in harsh daylight on top of an unrumpled bed. The next moment the curtains dropped and the scene was illuminated as it must have been the night before with the pink, intimate glow. The thought struck her that it must have looked like this when this woman died. She shuddered, stepped back and touched a half-empty bottle of champagne tipped over on the carpet. She stared at the familiar black label with its gold lettering and knew she would never drink Duval-Lercy again, that it would always bear the taint of this sordid and ugly scene, the seamy, unbeautiful side of sex. She crossed to the window, open narrowly but on the catch. She stared out, careful to touch nothing. It was a long drop. Too far for someone to jump or to have climbed and there was no convenient flat roof, ivy or drainpipe.

'Mike!' she shouted. 'Mike, I've found her. She's here.'

All the time she had stood in the bedroom the professional in her was noting down details: the single glass that lay on the bedside table, the copies of *Vogue* carefully placed around the room, the bunches and bunches of dusty silk flowers, cheap prints, the CD player still awaiting further instruction. *All By Myself ... Greatest Love Songs*, the scent of cheap, commercial air freshener and strong, assailing perfume, sweat. And the woman in her was revolted by the tackiness of the scene. There was no mistaking the function of this room. She shivered and watched the curtains move. Suddenly she felt faint.

'God.' Mike was standing behind her and she almost fell against the burly shoulders. 'What have we here? It's like a ...' He paused, stuck for words, and it was this inability to articulate that allowed her rank to surface, her faintness to evaporate and for her to begin studying the scene without the fog of emotion.

Yes – what did they have here?

A dead body – certainly.

A murder? Possibly.

A suicide? Again possibly.

An unexpected death – a sudden death. That much was certain. Marilyn Smith had not gone to bed expecting death to call.

'We need to ring the doctor,' she said.

'Dr Wilson?'

She shook her head. 'No – Dr Bose, the police surgeon. And we need the scenes of crimes officers and the photographer. I'll speak to the coroner,' she added. 'There will have to be a post-mortem.'

The wheels had to be set in motion. Sudden, so-far-inexplicable death. On the surface it was only the clothing that suggested anything but death by natural causes. Drugs – or suicide was a possibility. But Joanna knew she had to be aware. There might be, in the background, lurking, a murderer a little cleverer than the usual bloody thug who struck out in temper without forethought or planning. She glanced back at the bed. Judging by the seductive clothes it seemed reasonable to suggest that Marilyn Smith had been expecting a man last night. But if a man had come into this room his motive had been far from the romantic evening Marilyn had so obviously planned.

Champagne, soft music, perfume and seduction, then death. What had really happened?

# Chapter 4

Mike looked at her. 'So what now, Inspector?' he said. She knew he was testing her. It would all be reported later on in the pub. Guess what the stupid cow did then. Raucous laughter, incredulity . . .

She met the challenge. 'We use our eyes, Mike, and wait for Dr Bose. Come on,' she said. 'Look around. See what's here, staring at us.'

Mike blinked. 'I suppose it could be drugs,' he replied slowly. 'Ecstasy, cocaine, crack . . . Maybe she tried something' – his tone was dubious – 'and it didn't mix with the alcohol.' He paused for a minute then when she said nothing he spoke defensively. 'I can't see what else it could have been. We've had a good look round downstairs. There isn't any sign of a break-in.'

He glanced at the figure lying on the bed. 'She doesn't look as though she's been murdered.'

'No blood?' she asked sarcastically.

'Well . . . you know what I mean.'

She knew – only too well. The picture of murder was always spattered blood – not helped by the invasion of too many American movies. 'Go on,' she said.

He motioned at the bed. 'It looks neat,' he said. 'Too neat and tidy.'

Joanna nodded. 'Yes,' she said, then glanced at the bottle of champagne. 'Alone? Dressed like this?' She waved a hand at the black corseting. 'I suppose it's just possible.'

The body was not flung, not fallen but lying almost

comfortably on top of an unrumpled continental quilt. She knew that Mike's suggestion seemed the obvious one. Perhaps the SOCOs would find the twist of paper, the syringe, the usual signs. She walked round to the far side of the bed and almost kicked over a small, wicker wastepaper basket. Carefully she slipped on a pair of plastic gloves and picked something out.

She held it up. 'Look at this. Price labels, neatly cut off.'

She fished out another object, a polythene bag of the type expensive stockings are sold in. 'Mike,' she said slowly. 'It's all new. Everything she's wearing is brand new.'

She looked again at one of the labels in her hand. 'And expensive.' She dropped the labels into a regulation plastic bag.

'Bloody hell,' Mike said, over her shoulder. 'Eighty quid.' He whistled quietly.

Joanna looked with pity at the spreadeagled body, plump, white, undignified – a body dressed to attract which now merely repelled.

'Poor cow,' she said softly. 'Silk purses, sows' ears, oh, damn.'

Mike shuffled uncomfortably. 'Can't we cover her over, ma'am, make her decent or something?'

'Decent?' The word seemed out of place here, wrong – ridiculously so. She was almost tempted to laugh. Instead she spoke in a calm, flat voice. 'You know the rules,' she said. 'I don't want anything touched. And for the record, Sergeant, I think it would take a damned sight more than a clean sheet to make this woman decent.'

He met her comments with a mocking look. 'Judging her already, Inspector? And I think you've decided it's murder already without . . .' he wagged his finger in front of her face ' . . . a shred of evidence to suggest it.'

'Come on, Mike,' she said, waving an expansive arm around the room. 'There's everything to support it. This room feels like a . . .' she paused, 'a love nest, but the main character is missing. Where's the man – or sign of him?'

Mike chewed his lip. 'It's a drugs-related accidental death or an expensive suicide,' he said. 'The drama came from her.' He pointed his index finger straight at the dead woman's head. 'Like those film stars, ma'am. She couldn't quite make it in life so she dies the way she wants it – stylish.'

Joanna raised her eyebrows. 'Maybe, Mike, but let's not make premature judgements. They account for some of the biggest cock-ups the legal system has ever known.'

Mike scowled. His neck grew a fierce red and he mumbled something about seeing whether the police surgeon had arrived yet.

In a couple of minutes he was back, shaking his head. 'No sign.' He joined her at the window. 'Ma'am,' he said, 'No one came in this way. It's a clean sill, and no one could have hooked this window on the catch. This woman died alone.' His eyes looked hard and bright. 'Inspector,' he said softly, 'take my advice. Don't make a tit of yourself by making this one up to a full-blown murder investigation just to justify your pips. It's obvious what happened. It has to be drugs. She simply dressed up and OD'd.'

'Thank you, Mike,' she said. 'Thank you very very much. I really needed your advice. I don't know how I've got so far without it.'

He went red and looked around the bedroom.

Joanna felt suddenly overwhelmed by the claustrophobic atmosphere. 'It's so damned sordid, isn't it?' she muttered, but Mike's face was set.

'She died on her tod in this pathetic, make-believe love nest,' he said stubbornly.

She felt her shoulders sag. 'Oh – I hate that word.'

'What – tod?'

'No,' she said softly. 'Love nest,' and she winced.

A gust of wind threw the curtain upwards and she sniffed. 'Perfume,' she said. 'Can you smell it? Strong perfume.' She sniffed again. 'And no aftershave.'

But the scent brought her to a definite conclusion. 'She was waiting for a lover,' she said. 'He might not have turned up but she was waiting for a lover.'

Then, 'I want the scene of crimes men to strip this room completely. Take the house apart if necessary. I want to know who the man is. Tell forensics I want every bloody cell from that bed.'

She looked at Mike thoughtfully. 'All right,' she said. 'I may be wrong. I'm prepared to admit I may be barking up the wrong tree, but I bet my bottom dollar she had sex last night and I want to know with whom.'

Mike was near the door. 'So the missing lover is "our man", madam.' He spoke in an appalling mockery of a cheap New York twang.

'I intend to find out. And Mike,' she glanced at the set face, 'don't call me madam, will you? My name's Joanna. Every now and then you forget yourself and call me that. Just do it all the time, will you please?'

Mike shook his head. 'No,' he said simply. 'It's what you are. It's the recommended form of address. Page th—'

'Right.' Joanna blazed back at him. 'Now instead of hanging around here go and speak to her doctor. Perhaps he knows something that'll have some bearing on this. Heart complaint, diabetes or something.'

It had been a mistake to send Mike away. The room was silent. There was no movement except the fluttering curtains and the sharp click as the digital clock display numbers altered, ticking minutes away. Left alone she tried to ignore the still figure on the bed. But she shivered. Death should never be so sordid. Marilyn Smith deserved more dignity in her final pose. She glanced around, noting details . . . one bottle of sleeping pills – thirty dispensed. How many left? She opened the tiny drawer in the bedside cabinet. No birth control pills, or other contraceptive device. Of course, she thought, this did not necessarily rule out male presence.

Next she opened the larger drawers beneath and found nothing but layers of neatly folded underwear, plenty of black but nothing quite as exotic as the clothes she had died in. And the drawers in the fitted wardrobes revealed little else, various paperbacks, perfume, cosmetics.

But the cursory examination of the room failed to reveal two things – there was neither suicide note nor obvious sign of intent to commit suicide, nor evidence of the presence of another person. The central pillow on the bed had only one indentation in it. The bed itself was neat, unrumpled. Joanna peered at it. No hair, no parallel body shape in the bed, no sign that another man – or woman – had been here last night. She grimaced. The SOCOs would have to pay particular attention to the bed for it to surrender its secrets.

And then there was Ben. He had guarded his mistress and been loose in the house. And the interior doors had all been open. Whoever had come to Silk Street last night had been allowed in by Ben.

She stared out of the window, watching the froth of a flowering cherry dance in the breeze, and wondered. Yesterday Marilyn Smith might well have stood here and done exactly the same thing from exactly the same spot. She found the thought disturbing. This was always the worst aspect of a murder – connecting the victim with a living, breathing person. And now ... even more she found she could not stand the sight of those plump legs, splayed, ready for action. But she reached out and deliberately forced herself to touch the woman's arm. It was ice cold. Then she studied her face in minute detail. The skin was pale beneath the thick plastering of dark tan make-up that rimmed her face with a dirty tide-mark. Lilac eyeshadow lined into creases, and, most repugnant of all, the greasy red mouth, sagging open, giving a peep of surprisingly beautiful pearly-white teeth. Marilyn Smith had not been shy of the dentist. Joanna felt intrigued at this aspect of the dead woman's character.

'Definitely no signs of violence.' Mike's return made her jump. 'We've been right through the house. Everything's neat and tidy. No struggles. No blood anywhere.'

He carried on, ignoring her start. 'Her doctor is coincidentally Sammy Bose, so he can formally identify her when he arrives. I checked with his receptionist. He's on his way.'

He looked at her curiously. 'You look a bit green about the gills, madam. What's the matter? Don't like violent death?' He glanced meaningfully at the body. 'Now some unkind people might say if you're not fond of violent death maybe you should have done something else for a living.'

She shot a glance at him. 'Don't antagonize me, Mike. It won't help here.' She looked back at the body. 'This isn't violent death, anyway. Sudden, yes, unexpected, yes, but violent, no.'

He looked at her curiously. 'Does it upset you?'

She shook her head. 'No. It isn't the sudden death, Mike. It's the utter...' She struggled to find the right words to encompass the whole sordid atmosphere, still illuminated by the pink light from the two shades.

She suddenly snapped. 'Switch those bloody things off,' she said. 'It's the unexpectedness of it all.' She took a deep breath. 'She didn't expect to die. I'm sure of that.'

'Don't you believe it, madam.' He shrugged his shoulders. 'Women,' he said.

She couldn't think of an answer.

'Well...' He spoke again after a pause. 'You've had five minutes alone with the body. Who done it?'

She ignored the jibe. 'Who done what?' she said irritably. 'I'm not sure anyone did anything.'

'Tell me something, madam.' He grinned. 'Do women go to bed alone in that sort of get-up? Do they?'

'Well, I don't,' she said shortly.

His lips tightened. 'Or is it only when they're waiting for a lover? Or don't you know?'

'Let's wait for the doctor, Sergeant. Don't let your imagination run away with you.'

'Or perhaps,' he continued, 'it was the dog. Then again

maybe it was suicide. Or then again, madam, it is just possible it was murder.' He smirked. 'Have you looked for the knife in the back?'

'It's all possible,' she said. 'That's why we have post-mortems.' She glanced out of the window and caught sight of a white van pulling up. 'Let the photographer in, Mike. And, Mike,' she added, 'we'll need the next of kin.'

The indignity of death, she thought, as she watched the flash bulb explode time and time again. 'And don't forget the bed,' she said. 'I want a picture of that too.'

She wanted to remember this room in all its sorry gaudiness. Whatever had happened needed light shining through it – not sunlight, flashlight, or moonlight as it would have had last night when Marilyn Smith died, but the full unkind glare of truth.

The sound of tyres crunched through gravel and Mike crossed to the window. 'You'll soon have all your answers,' he said. 'Dr Bose has arrived.'

Sammy Bose had qualified in Nigeria and arrived in Leek eight years ago. At first the locals were suspicious, but Sammy's genial behaviour plus a certain clinical acumen and an outgoing personality had soon secured him the unenviable burden of police surgeon, and he spent many nights drawing blood from motorists who assured everyone, including the brick walls of police cells, that they had not had one drop over the limit.

They heard him whistling tunelessly as he mounted the stairs three at a time.

'Well, what have we here?' he said. 'Hello, you two.' He grinned at them and stared at the figure on the bed. 'I . . .' He seemed lost for words.

Joanna stepped forward. 'Dr Bose,' she said, 'can you give us a positive identification? Is this Marilyn Smith?'

Dr Bose nodded, still speechless, then he swallowed. 'Yes,' he said. 'I knew her quite well. But, God – who would have thought it? Excuse me,' he said. 'It's a shock. I never expected to see her like this.' He touched the stiff black lace of the basque.

They stood around the bed while Sammy Bose stared at the corsetry.

'God,' he said, 'this stuff looks expensive.' Then he grinned suddenly and his dark eyes sparkled. 'Well, who'd have thought it?' he said again. 'I would never have guessed Marilyn had such exotic taste in . . . Do they call this stuff underwear? Marilyn.'

He stared down at the still figure on the bed, her eyes looking at him dumbly from almost-closed lavender lids. 'Underneath the navy blue nurse's uniform she was wearing this sort of garb? I can't believe it. She always seemed such a . . .'

'Such a what?' Joanna prompted.

'I don't know.' The doctor rubbed his forehead with his two forefingers. 'One just doesn't imagine, you know.'

He looked at Joanna. 'She certainly had very expensive taste in underwear.' He touched the boned part that tapered the waist. 'Isn't this real silk?' He scratched his cropped head. 'I have to admit. I am puzzled. And this house,' he added. 'It's better than mine. How did she afford it? She was not married. I thought of her as rather a dangerous old maid.' He looked apologetically at Joanna.

'What on earth do you mean?' Her tone was sharper than she had intended.

'I don't mean to be rude.' Underneath the dark skin Dr Bose flushed almost purple. 'She was man mad,' he said simply, and quickly unpacked his equipment – gloves, thermometer, swabs.

The two police watched as the doctor made a thorough examination of the body. And it was thorough, hunting through her hair for signs of contusion, behind the ears, into the dead pin-point pupils, under and along the arms.

He looked at Mike. 'Help me roll her over, will you?'

Moving the clothing out of the way, he took a rectal

temperature, screwing up his eyes tightly as he read it. 'She died round about sixteen hours ago. Let me see ... That takes us back to around eleven last night.'

Mike looked sceptical – never a believer in science, he preferred to deal in what he considered hard facts. 'How accurate is that thing?' he said.

Sammy Bose grinned at him. 'A corpse's temperature nears the surroundings' by the end of the first day. It's pretty accurate. Divide the difference in body temperature by twenty-four and you have it – to within an hour or two. Basic principle of taking a large piece of meat out of a slow oven. Takes a long time to cool. See?' He gave a quick flash of pink tongue and very white teeth.

Joanna was silent. She knew where she had heard that analogy before. She could remember Mat explaining it to her six – seven – months ago ...

'We'll strip her completely, of course, at the PM, examine the clothing.'

Joanna nodded and watched him work until at last he stood up and she could begin to ask questions.

'Cause of death?' she asked casually.

Sammy Bose looked up at her. 'I haven't a bloody clue,' he said. 'Could be anything.'

'But you're her GP,' Joanna said.

'Listen, lady—'

'Inspector ...' Surprisingly it was Mike who said this, but Joanna felt annoyed rather than grateful. What did he think she needed? Some Sir Launcelot? She felt her mouth tighten.

'Inspector ...' Sammy Bose grinned. 'Sorry. I have to explain this. I am someone's doctor – yes. But I only see them professionally if they ask to see me. Otherwise ...' He shrugged his shoulders. 'She did not ask to see me. That's that. I saw her sometimes at the surgery – at medical lectures and meetings. She did not consult me professionally.'

Joanna felt at a loss. 'Was there anything wrong with her – heart?' she ventured.

Sammy Bose shrugged again. 'How should I know?' he said. 'As I've said. She didn't come to see me professionally. Look . . .' He stared straight at Joanna. 'Inspector?'

'Yes?' Joanna said testily. It had been a long day and it was nowhere near over.

'Inspector,' the doctor said. 'Get the body to the mortuary. Then you'll have to get a decent pathologist to dig around.' He looked across the body at her. 'You understand what I'm saying? I can't possibly issue a death certificate.'

'Dr Levin?' she asked.

'That's the one I was thinking of,' Sammy said, failing to notice her tentative tone, the faint flush. 'Get Mat Levin to do the PM.' He grinned reassuringly at her. 'He'll find something, I'm sure. Maybe drugs. I don't know. All I can tell you is this. She died here, without a struggle, on the bed, late last night.'

Joanna noticed Mike give a distinct smirk. 'And you can't suggest a cause of death?'

Sammy Bose shook his head. 'No,' he said. 'She was a slightly plump, otherwise healthy woman who died. That's all.'

But that was not all. And now, she thought, Matthew was to be involved – again. She gave a deep sigh and suddenly she didn't know whether to laugh or cry at the thought that she would soon be seeing him again.

Sammy Bose cleared his throat. 'If it's any help, Inspector,' he said, 'I think she probably died of natural causes. In fact the only thing I'm unhappy about . . .' he frowned, 'is the obvious – it's the clothes. If it wasn't for those . . . My God,' he said suddenly. 'It's a nasty thought – perhaps masturbation . . . I don't know. Maybe excitement brought on . . . Maybe you're right. Maybe her heart or her brain – possibly a subarachnoid haemorrhage. Sometimes the first you know of a weakness can be when the blood vessel bursts.'

He glanced at the bottle of champagne. 'And that doesn't help.'

'Do you know her next of kin?'

He frowned. 'No,' he said slowly. 'I don't think I ever heard her mention family. I don't think there was one.'

Joanna turned to Mike. 'We'd better get on with the PM before contacting the relatives.' Then, to Sammy Bose, 'OK to remove the body?'

He nodded. 'Fine. And you know what pathologists are like – the sooner the better. Fresh meat,' he said cheerfully.

'Right,' she said briskly to Mike, 'we can move the body but we'd better get the SOCOs over here. I want this place searched.'

# Chapter 5

For how long had the house been a prison? She put out her hand to touch the glass. Grey and cold, lifeless. An invisible barrier that held her inside these walls. She looked around the room, suddenly finding it unbearably large and open, and then back at the glass. The outside world seemed bright, a Disney view, intrusive. Angrily she pulled the curtains across with a snap. How dare it sit outside and stare in at her quiet privacy? She moved away from the window, backed towards the door and through into the hall. She liked it here, in her prison. It was cool and dull, and safe. The sun never came through. Some days she would sit at the foot of the stairs, clasping her knees with her hands. Then she would dream of Stevie. She smiled and hugged herself. 'Stevie,' she whispered. 'Stevie.' Suddenly she longed to touch all the familiar things, look out at the world through the bars of his cot, play with the soft, fluffy toys and hear the quiet tinkle of the musical box.

These were Pamella's anchors on normality . . . chairs and tables, old pictures and books . . . soft toys.

Joanna was sitting in the car with Mike Korpanski. In one hand she held a notebook, in the other a sharpened pencil.

'The place to start is the surgery,' she said. 'We can move from there to next of kin . . . friends . . . Perhaps from there we can find out – ill health, suicide intent . . .' She glanced at him.

'Murder,' he mocked.

'We can't rule it out,' she said. 'And someone was with her last night.'

He shook his head. 'We don't know that, ma'am.'

Joanna leaned forward and started the engine. 'We don't know it,' she said, 'but I certainly suspect it.'

The surgery was a modern, red brick, purpose-built building in the centre of town, with a raised roof which made it resemble a Chinese pagoda.

Joanna pulled into the car park, into a slot marked with a yellow sign. It read Nurse.

There were still a few patients sitting in the waiting room and as Joanna approached the hatch she was met by an anxious, questioning face. A tall redhead with pale freckles.

'Yes?'

Joanna showed her card. 'Detective Inspector Piercy,' she said. 'I'm afraid I have some bad news.'

She was ushered through the door and the two women listened to her, watching with shocked eyes.

'Dead?' one of them said incredulously, when she had finished. 'Marilyn dead?'

The smaller receptionist with thick pebble-lensed glasses frowned. 'How?' she asked.

Mike stepped forward. 'We don't know,' he said, 'yet. There'll have to be a post-mortem.'

The receptionist seemed to shrink. She sank down into a chair and passed a hand across her face, biting her lip hard and frowning.

'Do you mind if we ask you some questions?'

The two women looked apprehensive.

'When did you last see Marilyn Smith?'

The redhead answered. 'Yesterday. She came to work as normal. She left about . . .' She glanced at the other woman. 'What time was it, Maureen?'

'Just after five.'

Mike watched them both like a hawk, hungry for clues. Joanna sensed his impatience.

'What's your name, love?' he said.

'Maureen.' She warmed to the male charms of the tall policeman.

'Did she seem normal?'

She nodded, pale now and shocked. 'Yes. Exactly the same as usual.' She hesitated. 'How did she die?' she whispered.

'Did she have any health problems, Maureen?' Mike was turning on the charm full force.

Maureen shook her head. 'No. She always seemed all right.'

'I never even heard her complain of a headache,' the redhead butted in.

'What time was she due at work?'

'Half past eight this morning. She was never late. She took her work very seriously.'

'Did she have a boyfriend?'

Maureen shook her head. 'Not that I know of.' She looked at her colleague. 'I never heard her talk about one. Did you, Sall? At least . . .'

The redhead shook her head. 'Just Ben.' She giggled and the two of them flushed and exchanged some private joke.

'The dog?' Mike asked the question and they nodded vigorously.

'Devoted to him, she was.'

'He went everywhere with her.'

'Except work.'

'She shut him in a compound all day then took him out when she went home. Sometimes the neighbours used to call . . . say he was making a noise.'

'Like a burglar alarm, he was. Fierce dog.'

'I wouldn't have crossed him.'

Joanna frowned. 'Had she been depressed lately, trouble sleeping . . . Anything like that?'

The women shook their heads. 'Bouncy as ever. In

42

fact...' Sally leaned forward like a conspirator, 'She seemed extra pleased with herself lately. Chuffed. As if something was going to happen.'

'What did you think it was?' Mike asked.

'She sort of hinted it was something to do with a married man... someone with loads of money.' Sally's features sharpened. 'I've never known anyone love money so much.'

'Did she ever have time off for sickness?'

Again they shook their heads.

'Do you know who her next of kin was?'

Maureen paused. 'I know her mum was dead. That's how she got the money to buy the house in Silk Street. Left her a fair bit. But as for the rest of the family...'

Joanna listened. 'Father?' she ventured.

'No, he died years ago.' She looked at Joanna. 'I never heard her talk about brothers and sisters either. In fact... I don't think she had any family. Otherwise she wouldn't have got left all that money – would she?'

And with that question the interview seemed at an end, except for the last important fact.

'Which of you telephoned the police?'

'I did.' It was the redhead who spoke.

'Why?' It seemed an important point now. Why telephone the police when someone failed to turn up for work?

'A telephone call came to the surgery...'

'She'd rung a few times,' Maureen said helpfully, 'asking for Sister Smith. Then she said there was something wrong with the dog.'

'And who was it?'

'We think it was the next door neighbour. She's a bit strange,' Sally said apologetically. 'She's been weird ever since her husband disappeared. Her and Marilyn have had words on a few occasions.'

'What happened to her husband?' Mike asked innocently.

The two women looked at each other. 'He just went,'

Maureen said. 'According to Marilyn, one day he simply wasn't there.'

'People don't just disappear.'

'He did,' Maureen said stoutly. 'I'm telling you. One day he was there. The next day he'd gone.'

Joanna sighed. There was nothing here, she thought. No real clue to the nurse's death.

'Is it possible to speak to the doctor?' she asked.

Joanna instinctively liked Jonah Wilson. Fortyish with greying, untidy hair worn slightly long, touching the collar. A rough tweed jacket with sagging pockets leaking a stethoscope. His tie was not quite central and the end was frayed as were his shirt collar and both cuffs, and his trousers were baggy at the knees and lacked a crease. And as definitely as she knew she liked him she knew that Mike, standing stiffly at the door, did not.

'Good morning, Dr Wilson,' she said, sitting in the patient's chair on the other side of the desk.

He looked up and she caught an unexpected warmth in his smile.

'I didn't expect a woman when they said Detective Inspector.' He took off his glasses and laid them on the desk. 'I understand you have some questions to ask about Marilyn. Do you know how she died?'

Joanna drew in a deep breath. 'We're treating her death as suspicious,' she said, 'but I can tell you there was no sign of violence. And there was no sign of a break-in.'

The doctor smiled. 'No burglar would be such a fool as to try and get to Marilyn past Ben,' he said with a touch of humour. 'Devoted to her, the dog was. Protected her as though he were a paid bodyguard.'

Joanna nodded. 'What was Marilyn like?' she asked casually.

'Quite a good nurse,' he said. 'Energetic.'

'Honest?'

He closed his eyes. 'If I had thought she was not honest,' he said wearily, 'I would have given her the sack.

She was a paid employee, Inspector. I can tell you about her professional competence. But I can't tell you much else. Ask Maureen,' he said, 'or Sally. They'll know more.'

'Family?' Mike ventured from the doorway.

'I couldn't tell you,' he said, then touched his mouth. 'I seem to remember her having some time off. Mother's funeral?'

'When was this, sir?'

'I really don't know,' the doctor said. 'Three ... four years ago.'

'Could it have been five?'

He smiled vaguely. 'It could have been. I'm afraid I'm not very good with dates. Ask the receptionists,' he said apologetically.

'We have.' Mike's abruptness bordered on rudeness. The doctor seemed not to notice.

Joanna smiled encouragingly. 'Did you ever meet up outside work?'

The doctor shook his head. 'My wife and I lead exceptionally quiet lives,' he said quietly. 'My wife ... She isn't terribly well.'

'I see.'

'And where were you last night, Dr Wilson?' Mike again, firing questions from the doorway.

'I was on call.'

'And were you called out ...?' Mike drew out his notebook, 'between eleven and twelve?'

'I believe I was,' he said after a moment's thought. 'I had to travel out across the moors. Onecote,' he explained. 'Case of suspected meningitis.'

'And was it?' It was Joanna who spoke this time.

He smiled and ran his fingers through his hair. 'No,' he said.

She felt Mike looking at her and leaned forward. 'What was she like?' she asked again.

A veil seemed to drop over the doctor's face. 'You've already asked me. Marilyn was good at her job,' he said abruptly. 'Kind ... compassionate.'

45

Joanna's mind was drawn back to the obscene figure on the bed. The two did not match up. She glanced at Mike.

'She seemed to have a comfortable standard of living,' she said, 'for a nurse.'

The doctor shifted uncomfortably. 'I believe she owned a nice home,' he said. 'I was never inside it. I gave her a lift there once.' He nodded. 'It looked very pleasant.'

Again Joanna met Mike's sceptical glance. 'How do you think she afforded it, Doctor?'

'I have absolutely no idea.' Doctor Wilson picked up his glasses, fiddled with them, slipped them on. His hands were shaking.

'No idea?' Mike's tone was truculent.

The doctor lost his composure. 'I believe her mother died,' he said irritably. 'She inherited some money. Damn it . . .' He looked at both of them. 'I don't pry into my staff's financial affairs.'

'How much did you pay her?'

'Fifteen – sixteen thousand a year. I don't know the exact figure.'

'Who would?'

'My accountant.'

'Did she have an alternative source of income, Doctor?'

'I really don't know . . .' He glanced at his watch.

'Did you fancy her?'

Joanna gave Mike a warning glance.

'No . . . No . . . Of course not.' Jonah Wilson looked helplessly at Joanna. 'She was my nurse. We had very little to do with each other . . . We never saw each other out of work. We weren't friends or anything. We were colleagues.'

He was on the defensive. Joanna watched him carefully. There was distinct discomfort here. But it failed to hang together. She simply couldn't connect the figure lying spreadeagled across the bed with this softly spoken intellectual. If they were not exactly chalk and cheese they represented at least the difference between a cheap, sensational paperback and an encyclopedia. She watched the doctor and was puzzled.

He seemed to read her thoughts. 'I'm sorry,' he said. 'It's an awful shock. Yesterday she was here – working normally. I just can't believe she's dead. I'm sorry.'

Joanna smiled. 'That's all right, Doctor,' she said sweetly. 'Sudden death isn't pleasant, is it? But as soon as we have the results of the post-mortem we can probably drop the whole investigation.'

'Investigation?' He looked up.

'It's routine, Doctor,' Joanna said smoothly. 'I'm sure you understand – cases of sudden death.'

'Well, what did she die of?'

'We don't know – yet.' This time Mike's voice sounded almost threatening.

The doctor shot him a look. 'I have patients to see,' he said. 'Is there anything else?'

Joanna shook her head. 'No.' She stood up to leave, shook the doctor's hand. 'Thank you for your help, Dr Wilson.'

He gave her a shy smile. 'If it's any help, Inspector,' he said, 'I don't think she was the type to commit suicide and she was simply never ill.' He hesitated. 'But then it can be difficult to tell. As far as causes of death are concerned nature has a way of making the medical profession look foolish. Death doesn't always leave its calling card the week before. I think you'll find it was her heart.' He paused. 'Or a brain haemorrhage.'

'I expect so,' Joanna said soothingly.

She was almost through the door when the doctor added, 'Who will be performing the PM?'

She stopped in her tracks. 'I don't know,' she said. 'Probably the pathologist.'

Jonah Wilson nodded. 'I expect it'll be Mat Levin,' he said.

They let themselves out.

# Chapter 6

The following morning found Paul Haddon happily tend-
ing the body of Harry Twemlow. There was plenty to do,
cleaning and washing, some embalming. He carefully
drew up a syringe of formalin and injected it. The funeral
was set for Friday. He hummed as he worked. The relatives had expressed a wish to view the body – always a
challenge to an undertaker. But he was equal to the task.
Stage make-up, sparingly applied, the hair combed, the
face shaved. Decent clothing.

Then there was the inside of the coffin to be seen to.
Silk, red or blue. Sometimes he chose. Sometimes the
relatives expressed a preference. And plenty of flowers,
soft organ music. He glanced around the chapel of rest.
Lovely, he thought.


The post-mortem was set for ten o'clock that morning.
Joanna made her way to the Pathology Department of the
local hospital and parked her car next to the maroon BMW.

She sat for a moment, swamped by memories . . .
Matthew, grinning, jingling the keys. 'Guess what I've just
bought . . .' Pleased with his purchase, he had taken her
out for a joy ride, accelerating noisily up the M6 – until
a police car had flashed them across to the hard shoulder.
She remembered DS Mike Korpanski's shocked eyes as
he recognized her . . . By the fire in his stare she had known
explanations would be futile. And every time she saw Mike
Korpanski watching her she saw the same angry light.

'Joanna! Joanna!'

Startled, she roused herself. Matthew was rapping on the window, grinning. For a moment she stared, confused, memories mingling with the present, then she pressed the electric button and the glass slid down.

'Jo,' he said, 'what are you doing here? Surely you haven't come to see me?'

He bent in at the car window, his hand resting on the roof as she studied him. He was completely unchanged, the old, familiar Matthew, honey-coloured hair, broad shoulders, green eyes, tanned face with his frank, open expression, ready grin trying to suppress the gladness he felt in seeing her. She studied him and noted that today he was dressed typically casually, open-necked shirt, loose cotton trousers.

'I believe you have a PM booked for ten,' she said.

'The dead nurse?' He looked surprised. 'You're involved in that?'

'I'm heading the investigation,' she said with a hint of self-consciousness. 'Besides . . .' She smiled at him. 'I wanted to make sure you were doing your job properly.'

He touched her shoulder briefly. 'Jo,' he said warmly, 'I can't tell you how good it is to see you again. I've missed you.'

He opened the door and she stepped out. She was as tall as he was, and came level with his eyes. He stared at her, then smiled.

'It's no use you teasing me,' he said softly. 'I know darn well you're already feeling queasy at the thought of the craniotomy. Mind you, Jo,' his hand brushed her cheek and for a short moment her frown line was ironed out, 'you look bloody marvellous.'

She stood very still, tempted to snatch his hand back, hold it longer, harder against her cheek. 'So do you, Mat.' For a moment they stared at one another, oblivious to all around them, their only emotion joy in each other's company.

It was Joanna who moved first. With a quick movement she turned, bent down and locked her car. Then together they walked through the swinging doors into the hospital and turned down the long corridor towards the Pathology Department.

'Inspector Piercy,' he mused. 'So you got your promotion – at last. I read it in the paper,' he added. 'I'm proud of you, Jo.'

'Thanks,' she said. 'Yes, I got the promotion.' She couldn't resist adding, 'Life has to hold some compensations.'

He ignored the dig and disappeared into a cubicle to change. 'You deserved it after nobbling the Whalleys. Blood and thunder,' he said from behind the curtain. 'Leek's getting positively law-abiding.'

'Not too much,' she said, smiling. 'I don't want to be seconded to Manchester because there isn't enough work. I like it here. I've grown used to it.'

'Me too,' he agreed, emerging in theatre greens and white wellies. 'But perhaps we'd better reserve judgement on the quality of local law and order until after we've tackled this little problem.'

'This little problem' was wheeled in on a refrigerated trolley, smothered in a white sheet. Matthew lifted it. He stared at the black lace underwear, whaleboned figure, suspenders and the long stockings ending in cover girl high-heeled shoes. His eyes moved the whole length of the ladder. 'God,' he said, then glanced at Joanna. 'What a get-up.'

His eyes met hers and she couldn't resist a comment. 'Like a bloody fancy dress, isn't it?'

Matthew gave her a questioning look.

'Just right for a mistress,' she said sourly.

'Joanna . . .' he pleaded but she met his gaze unflinchingly.

'I've got the plastic bags,' she said. 'I think you'll have to cut the clothing off. We'll want it for forensics.'

Without another word he inspected the clothes, meticulously noting stains and tearing, and carefully cut them off and dropped them into the bags. Helped by the mortuary assistant he then measured the body, nape to feet, head circumference, dictating all the details into the small, pocket dictaphone.

Next he made a close inspection of the skin for contusions, tearings, took swabs of orifices, and inspected under fingernails for bloody pieces of tissue, or clothing from an attacker.

He turned the body over and spoke into his recording machine: 'Body unmarked – no sign of attack.' He glanced at her. 'Doesn't look like an assault,' he said. 'What were your thoughts, Jo?'

'I'm puzzled,' she said frankly. 'But I did wonder . . . drugs, poison? Perhaps . . . suicide? There were no signs of a break-in and the dog inside the house would have killed anyone who tried to get to her.'

She looked back at Matthew. 'She must have died of something, Mat.'

He grinned at her. 'Quite right,' he said. 'Let's see what pathology we can unearth.'

Now it was time for methodical work, deft hands sawing through the skull, search the brain – cross-sections in flesh and blood. Sternal split, the ribs pulled back to reveal heart, lungs . . . weighing each organ.

It was more than an hour later that he stood up.

'There's nothing here,' he said incredulously. 'I can't find a cause of death.' His face was troubled and set, and he stared abstractedly past her as though battling with a mental puzzle.

'Matthew,' she said gently, 'you're not making any sense. She must have died of something.'

'Viscera to Birmingham,' he said. 'They'll have to be analysed. It might be poison.' He looked dubiously at her. 'It could be – it's just that I don't think so. There's nearly always some sign – scent or discoloration, foam around the mouth, sometimes blisters if a corrosive substance was ingested. There's nothing. Not a clue.'

'But surely you would have picked up poison in the stomach?'

He shook his head. 'Not necessarily. Personally, I'd have plumped for natural causes. Ten pounds I'd have bet on a subarachnoid haemorrhage, some congenital weakness in the circle of Willis. But it wasn't there.'

She looked hard at him, chewed on her lip. 'I might have gone along with natural causes,' she said, 'if it hadn't been for the clothes... You saw them. She was togged up like a tart. It was all brand new. We found the price labels in the wastepaper basket. And then there was the room.' She frowned. 'Matthew – you didn't see it. Champagne, silk roses, pink lampshades. It was cheap, contrived – seductive – like a brothel.'

She found the words difficult to say to him of all people, recalling scenes she had set, rooms tidied, props placed for lovemaking – bottles of champagne in coolers, flowers, scented sheets.

Matthew met her eyes and she knew he was thinking identical thoughts. Mercifully he said nothing.

'Come on, Matthew,' she said softly. 'Women don't spend more than a hundred pounds on boned basques and négligés for nothing.'

He scratched his head in a confused gesture. 'Well, I don't think I've missed anything.'

'Intercourse?' she asked firmly.

'Again – I don't think so.' He paused. 'I can't see any semen or tearing and oedema – bruising. Of course I can't be one hundred per cent positive until the swabs come back.' He crossed the room, dictating into his tape recorder as he walked.

The police photographs were pinned up on an X-ray light and they looked at them... Marilyn, legs splayed, crude black underwear, make-up grotesque and bright...

'It isn't fitting together,' he said. 'It's like muddled pieces of two separate jigsaw puzzles... different shapes... different pictures. No sense,' he said flatly. 'No sense at all.

'And there's something else I want to show you,' he said, returning to the post-mortem table. 'She was a very expensive corpse.'

Joanna almost giggled. 'That has to be the first time I've ever heard a corpse described as expensive.' She bit her lip. 'Unless you count the cost of funerals. How can a corpse be expensive, Matthew?' she said. 'What do you mean?'

'This,' he said. 'Look.' He held back the ears, lifted the breasts, the chin, pointed out marks on the thighs – thin lines, paler than the surrounding skin, an asymmetrical lumpiness on the legs.

Joanna looked at him, puzzled. 'What are they?'

'This woman,' he said, 'spent a bloody fortune trying to look beautiful.'

'What?' She still didn't understand.

'Scars, Jo. They're Harley Street scars.' His enthusiasm for the job spilt into his voice. He loved finding clues. He was an expert in his field, a lover of puzzles.

And as she looked at his face, so absorbed and alight with enthusiasm, Joanna remembered a conversation they had once had long ago.

He had told her that he could usually tell the cause of death without making a single incision, simply by looking at the hands of a dead person: fingers clubbed with heart disease, distorted with arthritis, clutching in agony, mottled blue from poisons, nicotine-stained, cut or weathered, grazed in a fall, clutching a dozen clues beneath the fingernails. The list had been long and she had listened, half amused, until she had drawn a baptismal cross in wine on his forehead.

'OK, clever clogs,' she had giggled, and rolled to face him in the wide bed of a strange hotel. 'So why mutilate the corpse at all by doing a post-mortem?'

It had been one of their many warm, intimate, frank postcoital chats.

'Literal policewoman,' he had teased, wiping her hair away from her face. 'For the girls and the boys in blue I must always prove it.' He had kissed her and when his mouth was free had added, 'Beyond reasonable doubt.'

But she had known even then that it was the truth. Almost always he did know the cause of death by looking at his corpse's hands. And she had lain her head on the springy hair that forested his chest and listened to his heart's regular beating with fierce jealousy . . .

'So what about her hands?' she asked, coming back to the present and picking up a pudgy hand with short fingers, nibbled nails spotted with nail varnish.

He looked. 'The sign of a slut,' he said. 'She spent a bloody fortune on desirable underwear and plastic surgery and didn't even bother to put on new nail varnish.'

He smiled and his green eyes met hers, so she knew he recalled that conversation.

He took the hand. 'Work roughened,' he said, 'but she liked to think herself a lady. She took a lot of trouble that night, apart from the nails.'

'Just to die, Matthew?'

He turned and looked at her. 'You think suicide, Joanna?'

'What else?'

He left the table and washed his hands at a sink in the corner of the room, knocking the taps on with his elbows, peeling the surgeon's gloves from his hands.

'The scars were well hidden in hair lines . . .' He mused, rinsing his hands underneath the gush of water as he spoke. ' . . . Natural creases, tucked away in folds of skin, but once I'd found the first one I had a good hunt. She'd had the lot: some face reconstruction, nose job, breast augmentation—' He broke off for a moment and looked at her. 'You must have noticed the hard, pointed breasts. Typical fibrosis following silicone implants. All her teeth were crowned,' he continued, 'with pearly-white porcelain. And the lumpy look to the thighs – they almost always get that following liposuction. Yes,' he said again, 'that was a very expensive corpse, Joanna . . .' He looked at her. 'You realize we're talking about somewhere in the region of . . .' he stopped for a moment, mentally calculating, 'eighteen thousand or so. Harley Street plastic surgeon. Some top-quality work there. She was well off for a nurse.' He watched her carefully as he dried his hands on paper towels. She felt he was trying to tell her something.

'She would appear to be comfortably off,' she agreed cautiously, 'for a nurse.'

Matthew merely nodded. She looked carefully at his face. It still held that guarded, watchful look.

'So now where?' she asked.

Matthew cleared his throat. It was a habit he had when he didn't know what to say. 'I can't be sure,' he said and she wondered why he sounded so uneasy. Was it purely professional embarrassment at being defeated by a corpse? True, she had never known him stuck before; but was it so very important? Something was bound to turn up through the laboratory tests.

'There's only one – unusual – finding. She'd sweated a lot.' He looked at her. 'Was the room very hot – overheated?'

'No.' She paused. 'The windows were open. If anything, it was quite cool. And it certainly would have been last night.'

'Well, the clothes were still damp.'

'Did she have an infection?'

He shook his head. 'Nothing to support that at all.' He grinned at her. 'Coffee?'

Joanna walked along the corridor with him to his office and sat, perched on the edge of his desk, while he filled in the post-mortem forms.

'Mat,' she began, 'you realize this puts me in a tricky position. It means I have to put a full-blown murder investigation on hold. Discreet enquiries is about all I can get on with until you can find a cause of death.'

He cleared his throat again. 'Jo,' he said, 'if it's any help to you I very much doubt it's murder.' He paused. 'There is absolutely nothing to suggest it. I'd lay a bet on it that it was natural causes. Maybe she committed suicide. After all – she was a nurse. She would have had access to poisons.'

'And would you lay that same bet in front of the coroner?' she demanded.

He was silent, his eyes evasive, and she knew the answer. He would preserve his reputation in tissue paper, hedge his bets and reserve judgement. So why was he trying so hard to convince her?

'Well, to return to the facts,' he said after a minute. 'I'll know more this afternoon when I get some results back from the path lab, and even more by the end of the week when the results run on the viscera come back from the forensic lab in Birmingham.'

'Barbiturates,' she said suddenly. 'Sleeping tablets – the bottle I found on the bedside table.'

'I've bagged up all the stomach contents,' he said. 'We'll have a look what's in there. I'll know quite a bit later on today.' He hesitated for a while, frowning, and she chipped in sceptically.

'And the clothes, Matthew?'

'I'm inclined to think she died naturally while inhabiting some personal make-believe land, some fantasy land of her own. Hence the underwear, the champagne, the perfume, and so on.'

'So you noticed the perfume,' she said quietly. 'I might have known. But Matthew, if she died of natural causes why can't you find them?'

He had lovely eyes – green and very clear, fringed with thick dark eyelashes in spite of his blonde hair. Normally they held an honest, frank expression. Today they refused to focus on her. Instead there was a long, pregnant silence.

'What about lunch?' he said at last.

No, Joanna prayed silently to an unseen god, digging her nails into the palms of her hands: help me say no.

'We can visit the path lab after lunch, Joanna. If you were with me . . . we could call in together.'

'No, Matthew,' she said gently, her prayer answered. 'No. I have to report back to the station.'

She heard the hurt in his voice and saw it in his eyes but she was glad.

'All right,' he said quietly, 'if that's the way you want it.'

She picked up her handbag from the table. 'Matthew.' Her voice was soft, pleading. 'It isn't the way I want it, but it is the way it is.'

'Yes,' he said, suddenly irritable. 'I understand. But what have you found to replace what we had? Promotion?' He was following her to the door. 'Being an inspector – has that made up for it?'

'Of course not,' she said. 'Of course not, but at least I know where I am. At least what I have alone is honest. With you it was not.' She bit her lip. 'Jane haunted me,' she said finally. 'I hated her. It was all so deceitful. It took away my integrity. I began to despise myself.' She paused, remembering.

'Of course,' he said bitterly, 'now you're an inspector I suppose your . . . integrity . . . is so important.'

'It always was,' she said, 'but I overrode it.' She stared at him. 'But we both know it isn't really anything to do with my promotion. It's more to do with your wife.'

Matthew Levin groaned. 'Oh – so we're back to that, are we – petty jealousy.' He picked up his pad angrily. 'I'll let you have my report as soon as I've finished it. I'll ring you later with the rest of the results.'

Joanna walked out, letting the doors swing backwards and forwards . . .

The day was warm and sunny and Joanna felt hemmed in by the small office, even with the windows open. She picked up her jacket.

Mike was in the middle of eating a sandwich. He looked up as she stood in front of his desk.

'How did the PM go?' Pieces of bread sprayed out of his mouth on to the *Daily Mirror*.

'He can't find a cause of death.'

Mike swallowed his lump of sandwich and washed it down with a noisy swig of coffee. 'So where does that leave us?'

'I don't know,' she said. 'Confused, in a mess.'

She sat on the corner of his desk. 'It's difficult,' she

began. 'If you know you have a murder investigation you get the lot . . . extra men, time, money, facilities. In this case, until I know one thing or the other we're left in limbo.'

He nodded and took another bite from his sandwich.

'I wish there was something,' she said. 'Anything that might help.'

'Your pet pathologist didn't have all the answers, then?' There was a tightening around his lips.

She looked beyond him at the brick wall view through the window. 'He didn't have any of the answers,' she said.

'Oh dear.' He yawned and folded his newspaper. 'So what now?'

'We'll have to go back. Back to Silk Street – see if we can find anything there.'

# Chapter 7

It was time to join the SOCOs and spend the afternoon hunting through the house in Silk Street, but Joanna wasn't anxious to return. There was something unpleasant about the atmosphere – something cheap.

It was as they drove along the main Leek road that they passed a sign on the left, pointing the way to the Willow Veterinary Surgery.

On impulse Joanna touched Mike's elbow. 'Pull in,' she said. 'I'd like to see Ben.'

Mike gave her a swift, pitying look. 'Bloody typical,' he said. 'Illogical. What's the point of going to see the dog? He can't tell you anything.'

'I know,' she said frostily, but she was unable to explain logically why she wanted to see the Alsatian again – except that whatever had happened on Tuesday night he must have seen it. Perhaps he could even have prevented it. He had been closer to the dead woman than anyone she had yet found.

Roderick Beeston was standing in the yard, in his jeans, wellies and green oilskin. His hands were deep in his pockets as he watched a dog vomiting. 'Possible sheep worrying,' he said, without looking up. 'Farmer tried to shoot him – missed, thank God. It was a twelve-bore, double-barrelled job. Would have made quite a mess of this little chap.'

He scratched his greying beard, his face set and angry. 'Have you any idea, Inspector, what a mess this creature would have been in if the farmer hadn't been drinking so much home-made parsnip wine he couldn't stand up, let alone shoot straight?'

'No.'

He looked up then. 'And what brings you here, Inspector?'

But before she could answer, his attention was diverted by a quick movement of the dog's flanks as he retched and vomited.

Joanna paused while the vet peered at the vomit, found no sheep fur then grinned at the dog. 'OK, Hannibal,' he said, scratching the top of the dog's head, 'looks like you're innocent. Good dog.' He held the dog's head as it retched again. 'Good dog,' he said again. Hannibal's tail wagged feebly as his brown eyes met those of his deliverer.

'Farmers shoot first, look for the evidence later,' the vet said. 'Damned good job you don't do the same, Inspector.' He gave a loud, explosive laugh but sobered up quickly. 'I wonder who you'd have pointed your gun at over the Marilyn Smith affair.'

Joanna opened her mouth to speak, thought better of it and said nothing.

The vet turned his attention back to the dog. 'This stuff makes them feel pretty grim,' he said, tickling the dog's proffered tummy. 'But not half as grim as a bullet in the brain. Still . . .' his voice was indulgent, 'nasty being sick, old thing. But it was worth it, wasn't it?' The dog's tail wagged again, then he put his head down on his paws, exhausted.

'Now then, Inspector, what can I do for you?' He looked at her and she saw his eyes were very bright blue, intelligent and humorous, his eyebrows bleached almost white from the weather.

'I came to see how Ben was.'

The vet looked pained. 'I've put him to sleep,' he said quietly. 'He was distressed when he woke up.' He tugged at his short, neatly trimmed beard. 'Marilyn spoke to me about him some time ago. She wanted him put down if anything happened to her. She felt it would be better for Ben.'

He looked at Joanna defensively. 'It isn't unusual, Inspector, for a well-loved pet to be put to sleep when the owner dies.' He frowned. 'I don't like it any more than you do. But that's what she wanted.'

'She left instructions for Ben to be put down when she'd had him from a puppy?'

The vet looked at her. 'Ben was about a year old when she got him,' he said. 'A friend let her have him – couldn't cope with such a boisterous dog.' He smiled. 'And Ben was boisterous. He was a wild dog in many ways. When he came round he was snarling and snapping. I honestly don't think anyone else could have controlled him. He would have attacked us if we had let him out of his cage.'

She left the vet's with a feeling of pity for the dead Alsatian. Ben had been fine with his mistress. There had been no complaints of attacks. She had run her own check on the dog and he had a clean record. And his arranged destruction gave an unsavoury angle to Marilyn Smith's character. She had cared about Ben, yet she had instructed that he be destroyed in the event of her death. Joanna climbed back into the car.

Mike was watching her. 'Did the dog bark out the name of the murderer in Morse code?' His face was relaxed and mocking.

Words of an old pop song flitted into her mind . . . 'You always hurt the one you love . . .'

'Ben's dead,' she said. 'Marilyn had asked the vet to put him down if anything happened to her.'

Mike was staring ahead. 'If anything happened to her?'

She was silent for a moment and he spoke again. 'She *expected* it?'

'I don't know.'

He swung the wheel of the car. They were turning into Silk Street.

'Beeston could have got past the dog,' he said.

She didn't even feel the remark worthy of comment.

As their car crunched up the drive Joanna took a good long look around her. The Astra sat in the drive, still parked where Marilyn Smith had left it the night she had died. It bore a violent green tape around it, left by the SOCOs following their check. So far they had turned up nothing – not one single hair that belonged to anyone but the dead nurse. Therefore, by the law of forensics, no one else had been there. Joanna looked at the car resentfully. Was the scene worth sealing off? Was there anything here that the house could yield ... one single piece of forensic evidence that would link someone – perhaps a killer – to this house? Or had she died alone?

'I think we'd better impound it,' she said, 'until we have an idea of what we're up against.'

They walked slowly towards the front door. The front garden was not very pretty, mainly paved, with large tubs of waving daffodils and scarlet tulips. The dead nurse had been an enthusiastic if gaudy gardener. Joanna looked up. All four of the front-facing windows were UPVC with mock Georgian glazing bars, strips of gleaming white plastic cased within the two panes. Again the effect was expensive and bright. Putting together the value of the property with the thousands Matthew had said she must have spent on plastic surgery, trying to look beautiful, Joanna assessed the dead woman's income as being far in excess of that of the average nurse. There was no evidence of hardship – no peeling paint, neglected window frames. The Astra in the drive was top of the range. And it was only a year old.

The SOC team were sitting in the squad car, eating their sandwiches as Joanna opened the front door.

'Found anything?' She donned the paper suit and over-shoes and one of them shook his head.

'Not a bleedin' thing,' he said grumpily, then added, 'ma'am.'

The clock struck suddenly. Joanna jumped then stared at it.

'It's uncanny,' she said. 'It always seems to strike just as we walk in.'

'It's the top of the hour, ma'am,' Mike pointed out with a trace of sarcasm in his voice.

She wheeled around. 'I didn't exactly mean that,' she said. 'The clock. It draws attention to itself. It simply doesn't belong, does it? It isn't gaudy or showy or bright. It's something else.' She frowned. 'It doesn't fit in with that...'

'Painted tart we found upstairs?'

Joanna was silent, angry with Mike for voicing thoughts she would not have uttered out loud. She pushed open the door and they moved into the sitting room. The bright, painted china dancing ladies stared at them with dumb eyes. Joanna picked one up.

'About how much do these things cost, Mike, do you think?'

'I can tell you exactly. One hundred and sixty-seven pounds fifty,' he said grumpily. 'I bought one for my wife's birthday.'

She set it down again and glanced around until her eye was caught by another incongruous piece. She crossed the room towards a small antique bureau, beautifully inlaid with a stag hunting scene, ivory, ebony and other pretty woods. She spotted the white dust of fingerprint powder on its surface.

'Looks like the SOC officers have already been here,' she said. 'It's a good surface. What did they find?'

'The only clear fingerprints they found were Marilyn's.' Mike glanced at his notebook. 'And that goes for practically the whole place.'

She glanced at him. 'Others?' she queried.

'Nothing recognizable. She did live alone,' he said defensively.

Joanna turned to him. 'Mike,' she said. 'How many women do you know who live alone?'

He flushed.

'Without any man even in the background?'

His face and neck turned a deeper red. 'At one time,' he muttered, 'I would have said only you.'

She hardened her jaw. 'Well, that just proves a point,' she said sharply. 'Practically every woman has someone. And some women manage to keep them hidden from public sight.'

'You think a married man, then, ma'am?'

'Possibly,' she said coolly. 'And this woman,' she jabbed her finger on the bureau, 'if she did have a man – and circumstances suggest she did – she managed to conceal it rather well, don't you think? The grandfather clock, this bureau, two expensive antiques. Perhaps they were presents from a lover?'

For answer Mike gave a loud and sceptical snort.

The bureau had been forced open by the SOCOs. As everywhere else in the house, the contents of the desk were tidy and organized.

'Know anything about antiques values, Mike?'

'No,' he held up a bundle of receipts, 'but these might answer some of your questions.' He couldn't resist smirking. 'And in answer to your question, ma'am, there wasn't a boyfriend. She bought them.'

Joanna glanced through them. 'One thousand three hundred pounds – for a clock? Is this how much they cost?' She stared at the sergeant. 'Mike,' she said, 'where did all the money come from?'

He shook his head.

'And this – three thousand for this tiny bureau?' She gave a sudden smile. 'Have nurses had such wonderful pay rises?'

Mike gave a short laugh. 'My wife's a nurse,' he said grumpily. 'I can tell you how much she earns and it wouldn't buy the contents of the garage.'

Joanna held up another of the receipts. 'They're all from the same place. Do we know this shop?'

Mike scowled. 'Do I know it?' he said furiously. 'We

never could get anything on clever little Mr Grenville Machin and we've been watching him for three or four years. He's as crooked as a nine pence piece. He's become a millionaire in a blink of an eye, lives in a bloody mansion. He's known by all the police in this area. God only knows what rackets he's into – drugs, organized crime – almost certainly acts as a fence. We even managed to get him on an attempted murder charge, but . . .' He walked across to the window and stared out. 'He got off,' he said. 'People like him always do. They can afford the best lawyers. He got a QC from Manchester who got him off scot free – for a fee. We ended up looking bloody silly in court.'

Joanna watched him curiously and wondered why Mike was so bitter about the case. What was the degree of his involvement?

'Tell me,' she said.

Mike turned and looked at her bitterly. 'Another time, Inspector,' he said, 'but I can tell you that man made a damned monkey out of me and for that I'll never forgive him. And within the law I can tell you something else. For all your clever ways, Inspector Miss Madam Piercy, you'll never pin anything on Grenville Machin. He's too clever even for you, even for this super-race of females. Men like that' – he spat the words out – 'the law can't touch them. And that's the dog-end of this job. The law can't or won't touch them. It's even worse than working under women, madam.'

Joanna stared at the furious policeman, more hurt than she would have thought possible. She stood for a moment, then shrugged. She turned her attention away from him and picked up a sheaf of letters, glancing at the signature on the one on top . . . 'Love, Mum'. She glanced at the date. 'Didn't someone say Marilyn's mother was dead?' she asked.

Mike nodded. 'I think the doctor's receptionists did.'

She held up the letter. 'The date on this is last week,' she said.

Mike stared at her. 'Address?'

'Cardiff. Why say her Mum had died? Obviously,' she said, 'to explain away the money.'

She would go through the letters later, in her own time. For now she wanted to get on with her search of the dead woman's house, and leave, as soon as possible.

But as she wandered into the kitchen she pondered Mike's bitter words and she felt that old, familiar quickening of the pulse she had first experienced when reading as a child, 'The game's afoot, Watson.'

Here was someone else in the incomplete picture of Marilyn's life: a local man with criminal tendencies, someone who believed he was above the law. Was he also conceited enough to commit murder and believe he could get away with it? And was he intelligent enough to have killed Marilyn without detection?

She stood, leaning against the doorway. 'Mike,' she said. 'Did you say you had him on an attempted murder charge?'

'Woman shot,' he said. 'Old girlfriend. They had a row. He said the gun went off by accident. Like hell it did. She got blasted in the arm.' He stared at her. 'She nearly lost it. If it hadn't been for a 999 call, a quick ambulance with paramedics and a damned skilled surgeon, she might have died.'

She pushed her hair back off her face. 'So you had the evidence.'

Mike looked even more sour. 'We thought we did. She made a statement – said he'd told her he'd kill her.'

'Then surely she testified?'

'They got to her first,' he said. 'She withdrew it, denied they had been rowing at all, said it had all been an accident, that she'd asked him to show her how the gun worked. By the time we'd finished we didn't even bother getting her on a charge of obstructing the police. It wasn't worth it,' he ended bitterly. 'We didn't have a chance. With our chief witness changing her statement it would have got thrown out of court. We couldn't even make stick a charge of malicious wounding. Would you believe it, the crafty bastard even had a bloody licence for the gun.'

'What happened to her afterwards?' she asked, curious. 'Is she still living in Leek?'

'She went off to open a restaurant in the Costa del Sol.' He blinked. 'With her little boy. Knowing the way he works, they threatened the child. And I wonder where all the money to open the restaurant came from.' His face was red and angry. 'A lot of the trouble in this peaceful little town,' he said, 'can be traced straight back to him. He's in it right up to his little squirt's neck.'

He paused for a moment. 'Someone did get to him once . . .' He reflected. 'Threw him off the edge of Ludd's Cave. Unfortunately, he lived.'

Joanna was silent, then she looked at Mike. 'How is it I haven't heard of him?' she asked.

Mike looked at her thoughtfully. 'He's been quiet for a year and a half.'

She frowned. 'Could that be anything to do with Marilyn?'

He shook his head. 'Probably planning something,' he said. He paused, then looked at her as though debating whether to bring up a subject. 'Do you ever have nightmares, ma'am?' he asked.

She shook her head. 'Nothing too troublesome.'

'I'll tell you my nightmare,' he said, his dark eyes glinting. 'We're surrounded by moors. Has it never struck you, Inspector,' he asked, 'all these miles and miles of moorland? They're snowed up for half the year, inaccessible. Roads – they hardly touch the edges. The ground's soft, peaty. It's one of my nightmares. If there were a hundred bodies hidden up there we might never find them.' His fists were clenched, the great veins standing out on his thick neck.

'Come back to the case, Mike,' she said softly. 'Marilyn Smith was found, not on the moors but here, in the centre of town, tarted up to the nines in her own bed, behind her locked front door.'

She saw him flush then and she could have bitten her

tongue off. Damn. Why hadn't she said something less conflicting? He had at least shared a confidence and all she had done was to mock it.

'But he is connected, isn't he?' he mumbled.

As though in answer the grandfather clock in the hall clanged the half-hour. Mike turned. 'All these antiques,' he said. 'They came from him.' He looked around him. 'They hardly belong, do they, ma'am? They stick out like duchesses in a brothel.'

Joanna was silent, deep in thought. It was possible that Grenville Machin was the man Marilyn had been waiting for. In that case a felony was surely more probable than simply possible. And where an acquaintance of a man suspected of attempted murder dies unexpectedly . . .

She examined the kitchen minutely. New white units would have gleamed, had it not been for the layer of dust and grime. Marilyn had not had too much of a conscience about housework. She pulled open the dishwasher door. It was full of dirty dishes. Marilyn had eaten well the night she had died. On the side lay the remains of a meal of steak, chips, tomato sauce and a dish of fruit salad with an empty carton of double cream. Recalling the corpse padded with fat, Joanna decided Marilyn had not battled against the flab.

Mike joined her in the kitchen. 'Nice,' he said appreciatively. 'Wouldn't mind a kitchen like this myself, and Fran would love it.' He wrinkled up his nose. 'She'd keep it a bit bloody cleaner, though.'

'Yes, but again,' Joanna said, 'money.'

It was an hour later, after systematic searching of the downstairs rooms, that Joanna looked at Mike. 'I think we'd better start upstairs,' she said.

The curtains had been tied back, the bed stripped down to the mattress and the bedding sent to forensics. The room had lost its seductive, harem look and looked and smelled exactly like any woman's bedroom, tidy, clean, perfumes, cosmetics . . . Pink and lace and Doulton dancers.

'No contraceptives,' Joanna pointed out when they had hunted through the drawers and the fitted, mirrored wardrobe.

'No more of those saucy négligés either,' Mike said.

'No, she seems to have had just the one outfit.'

'For the one night.'

'And no love letters either,' Joanna said.

'What on earth was the significance of the new clothes?'

Joanna sighed. 'It beats me.'

Mike's dark eyes met hers. 'Suicide,' he said. 'It has to be.'

'Then how?' demanded Joanna. 'And where's her reason, her farewell to the world?'

'Maybe,' Mike spoke slowly, 'maybe she wrote to her mother.'

Joanna nodded. 'Mike,' she said. 'Maybe you're right. It's possible. OK. We'd better send the local force round to tell her and warn her we'll be coming down.'

Mike nodded.

'Go back to the station,' she said. 'We'll go to see her tomorrow. For now I think I'll have a word with Mrs Shiers, the next door neighbour.'

'You think it was her who rang the surgery?'

'It has to be.' She frowned. 'What do you know about her, Mike?'

'That she's a well-known eccentric,' he said. 'And, as you learned this morning from the doctors' receptionists, that her husband vanished without trace a few years back.'

Joanna looked up. 'So you know about that?' she said.

He nodded. 'She never reported him missing,' he said. 'Local belief was that he'd left her for another woman.' He scratched his chin. 'People gossiped but we never made anything of it. There was no suggestion of foul play at the time.'

'Perhaps we'd better look into it, Mike,' she said, 'in a gentle, probing way. Softly softly ... It's possible there's something there.'

69

'Perhaps we should,' he agreed. 'But what gets me is why she hasn't come across and spoken to us. Why does she just sit there, spying on us? She knows we'll have to talk to her sooner or later.'

'Some people,' Joanna said, 'are frightened of "getting involved" with the police. They're worried suspicion might end up at their door.'

'Especially if they've got something in their past,' Mike said grimly.

# Chapter 8

A mental picture of Evelyn Shiers had formed in Joanna's mind. Nosy, timid . . . with maybe a guilty conscience?

The reality was nothing like that. A frightened fox, ginger bristles twitching, opened the door. Joanna was glad she had left Mike behind. Burly policemen frighten old women, who are never quite sure whose side they're on.

'Mrs Shiers?'

The woman twitched.

'I'm Detective Inspector Piercy. I've come to ask you a few questions about your next door neighbour.'

The woman twitched again, gave a loud gulp then said defensively, 'I don't know anything. I don't know why you want to see me. I hardly knew her.'

Joanna smiled encouragingly. 'Only a few questions, Mrs Shiers. It won't take long.'

Grudgingly, Evelyn Shiers opened the door.

Joanna saw salt-and-pepper hair, a faded redhead, bristles on her chin, pale eyes and a flowered overall on a thin frame. She followed her into the small living room. Two ginger Toms occupied the sofa of a brown three-piece suite. She selected the armchair and sat opposite the grey eye of a television.

'It was you, wasn't it, who rang the doctor's surgery yesterday?' Joanna spoke gently. Evelyn Shiers responded.

'I didn't know what to do,' she said. 'I thought she . . .' She glanced to her left, in the direction of the nurse's

71

house. 'I thought she would think I was interfering.'

'Did she ever accuse you of interfering?' Joanna asked casually, as though the answer was unimportant; but it was important. Was the woman a snoop?

Evelyn Shiers' eyes flickered. 'She liked to keep herself to herself,' she said quietly.

Joanna waited, sure the woman would speak again, and she did.

She leaned forward in the chair, knotting her fingers together. 'She's dead, isn't she?' There was no mistaking the eagerness in her voice. 'I mean . . .' Her voice trailed away. She looked embarrassed.

Joanna nodded. 'Yes,' she said. 'She's dead.'

Mrs Shiers stood up abruptly, turned away and stared out of the window. 'I should have rung earlier.'

Joanna stood too. 'It wouldn't have made any difference. She was already dead by the time morning came.'

The neighbour's eyes widened. 'Lying there dead,' she said, 'while I was having my breakfast?'

Joanna nodded.

The woman sank back on to the sofa, burying her face in her hands. She gave a long shudder, then looked up. 'Horrible,' she said.

'Mrs Shiers,' Joanna said slowly, 'do you have any idea if anyone might have visited the house on Monday night?'

She shook her head. 'No,' she said. 'They wouldn't have got past Ben.' She stared. 'What do you mean,' she said, '*visited* the house? Do you mean someone – killed her?'

'We don't know.'

'Well, was she ill?'

'We don't think so.'

Evelyn Shiers screwed up her face tightly, concentrating hard. 'Don't you do post-mortems and things?'

'They didn't find anything.'

'Nobody came to the house.' She was stroking her chin, had found one sharp bristle and was fingering it. 'Ben would have barked. I would have heard him. Nobody came.'

Joanna sat down again. 'Mrs Shiers,' she said. 'What was Marilyn like?'

Evelyn began to bob her head quickly up and down . . . up and down, like a hen. Joanna watched it and recalled where she had seen this habit before. It had been in an old folks' home and the woman, she had been told, had been quite demented. She waited for Mrs Shiers to talk.

'She was a nasty thing,' she said slowly. 'Nasty. Cruel.' She smiled. 'You can tell that from Ben. When he came he was a quiet dog, affectionate. I saw him in the garden.' She looked up. 'I used to pat him then.' She paused for a moment and then continued. 'He changed. He got wild. She used to taunt him, you see, tease him, and gradually he got like that . . . wild. I used to hide when Ben was out.'

'You never complained about him?'

Evelyn Shiers blinked. 'What's the point?' she said. 'Who'd listen to me? You haven't got the time.'

Joanna was silent.

'It wasn't the dog, was it, that killed her?'

Joanna shook her head. 'No,' she said simply. 'It wasn't the dog.'

Evelyn Shiers bobbed her head up and down again. 'I didn't really think it would be,' she said. 'Worshipped her, Ben did. I think maybe that was the problem. You see – there was just the two of them.' She thought for a minute. 'Just the two of them . . . He was upset that morning. I never heard him whining like that before. In real distress, he was. Sounded real mournful.'

Joanna puzzled over the significance of the dog. How much did Ben know? Then she remembered. Ben was dead too. She sat in the armchair and stared out of the window at a few dying primroses struggling against the weeds.

Evelyn Shiers followed her gaze. 'Cat pee,' she said calmly. 'No plants are fond of it.'

Joanna returned to the subject of Marilyn. 'Did she have many friends?' she asked.

'Not her.' Evelyn pursed up her lips. It gave her a tight, spiteful look. 'Not her. She pretended. Marilyn liked to pretend that she had lots of friends – especially men friends. But she didn't really. She hardly ever went out and I only saw one or two men come to the house. And they never came again. She'd fool herself, tell me about hotels and restaurants she'd visited. But it was all lies. She never went anywhere.'

'The men who came to see her . . .' Joanna persisted. 'Who were they?'

Evelyn thought for a minute. 'That antique fellow,' she said. 'He came to bring furniture once or twice. Hardly stayed a minute.'

'When was this?'

'Months ago.' Evelyn shrugged her shoulders. 'It was a long time ago, anyway. And he never stayed. The van pulled up. He offloaded the piece and then he was off again. Quick as anything.' She gave a surprisingly coarse cackle. 'Too quick for a lover.'

'Anyone else?'

'She said' – Evelyn's eyes narrowed – 'she said her boyfriend was married. I never believed her.'

Joanna felt cold. Something had touched her in the bedroom, the fornicating pose, the clothes meant to seduce. All for a married man? 'Did she say anything more about him?'

'He didn't exist,' Evelyn said. 'There was no married man.'

'Any cars ever parked outside?'

'I'm telling you . . .' Evelyn was almost shouting. 'There weren't anyone.'

Joanna dropped the subject. She looked through the window. She could see the corner of the red brick house. 'Nice place,' she said. 'Expensive house for a nurse to buy.' She waited for the other woman to find her cue.

'Now there I can help you,' Evelyn said. 'Her mother died. She came into a lot of money. A few years ago.' She too looked at the house.

'How do you know her mother died?'

'She told me,' Evelyn said. 'She told me all about it.

74

Ill she was, in a nursing home. Draining away all her inheritance. Then she died – quite suddenly. Marilyn even went away for the funeral. In black,' she added defensively. 'In black.'

Joanna recalled the letters. Number 6 Bute Street hardly sounded like a nursing home. And Marilyn's mother, she was sure, was not dead.

'When did you last see Marilyn?'

'Monday,' Evelyn said without hesitation. 'She didn't see me. I saw her through the window, getting into that car of hers. She was in her uniform. She looked sort of – pleased with herself – jaunty. Made a lot of noise with the engine. She knew it annoyed me,' she said simply. 'That's why she did it.'

The police had names for people like this. Natural victims . . . blame themselves for all that goes wrong, expect people to pick on them, wait for trouble. And hey presto, Joanna thought, trouble hunts them out as though it could smell them.

'Then what?' she asked.

'She sat in the car with the radio on very loud. She liked to do that. It made Ben mad. It upset him. She loved to tease him, you see. She loved to see him upset. He'd foam at the mouth – bark – try to jump over the fence.' Evelyn glanced at Joanna. 'He couldn't, of course. The fence was too high. Then she'd laugh and mock him, sometimes dangle a bone over the fence and laugh while he tried to catch it in his teeth.' She blinked. 'There was a very mean side to Marilyn, Inspector,' she said. 'She could be cruel . . .'

'You live alone, Mrs Shiers?' She changed tack.

An expression of extreme distaste crossed the woman's face. 'I do,' she said.

'A widow?'

'My husband and I are . . .' there was a quick, hesitant pause, 'separated.'

Joanna drew out her notebook and pencil. 'For how long?' She looked up, waited for the woman's reply.

75

'Four years.'

'And where is he now?'

Evelyn looked furious. 'I don't know,' she said. 'I don't care. He isn't here.'

'So where is he?'

Now the look of the frightened fox was back. She was cornered. 'I can't tell you . . . I don't know where he is.'

Joanna watched the bristles on her chin. Her head jerked to and fro. Evelyn Shiers was rattled.

She sighed. More questions . . . more investigations. And she had the feeling it would all be very hard work. But not now. She stood to leave and watched the other woman's shoulders drop in relief.

'By the way,' she said at the doorway. 'We don't know how Marilyn died. Lock your doors, Mrs Shiers. If you see anything—'

'What sort of thing?' the woman demanded.

'Anything. And ring us immediately, if you do.' Joanna gave her the number of the police station and her own extension number. 'I'm Detective Inspector Piercy. And I'll be interested if you remember anything that could have a bearing on this case.' She opened the front door. 'I'll probably call round again.'


'Is that the truth, then, Mike?'

They were sitting in her office, drinking coffee.

'Was she just a plump, lonely woman who spun stories, lived in make-believe land, dressed to kill and died?'

He was frowning. 'It could be,' he said cautiously. 'There was nothing in the house to suggest anything else.'

'Where did all the money come from? The antiques . . . plastic surgery . . . the house? Her mother isn't dead, is she? So she wasn't left anything.'

Her hand rested on the pile of letters. 'Maybe we'd better read these.' She picked one up and handed him another. Her eyes wandered down the page. 'A little more money . . . I saw the vicar calling in next door last Wednesday. I don't think it's quite nice for him to call,

76

so late at night, a man of the cloth ... and she was looking very tidy ... Mrs Tolley, three doors away goes out every single Friday night, you know, Marilyn. She thinks I don't see but a car drops her off. I went for a walk myself last Friday just to the end of the road. To get a bit of air. And there he was – the one man in the car. Nobody I recognized. But if Mr Tolley should find out ...'

Joanna slammed the letter down in disgust. She could sense the relish. She picked up another and read more. There were pages and pages of gossip, prying, intimate and insinuating. She dropped the letters and looked at Mike.

'What utter—'

'Crap,' he said. 'She was just a nosy old bag.'

'But she's alive all right – alive and prying. Like mother like daughter?'

'Perhaps we'll find out more tomorrow.'

She toyed with her pen before mentioning yet another point which had been bothering her. 'And what about the dog, Mike? I don't believe anyone could have got past Ben.'

'Maybe if she'd let someone in,' Mike said slowly, 'the dog would have been calmed.'

'Maybe.' She was not convinced. 'But would it have let someone out without Marilyn's presence?'

She looked at him. 'A lover? But no intercourse.'

'Lesbian?' he queried, then gave a lopsided grin. 'There wouldn't be any need for contraception then.'

'Yes,' she said. 'True.'

She cupped her chin in her hand, elbows on the desk, and gazed at Mike. 'What do we go on?' she said. 'The absence of a cause of death or the absence of signs of foul play?'

Mike was silent for a minute and then said carefully, 'The only reason we believe it was foul play is her clothes. We know she liked attention. What if she wore them to gain it?'

She sighed. 'I don't know ...'

She doodled for a while on the pad. 'Any more thoughts, Mike?' Before he had a chance to answer she gave a wry smile. 'Sod's law,' she said. 'I could really have done with a nice, clean murder for my first serious investigation. What's this going to amount to? A missed diagnosis? At best a sordid little sex crime.'

He stood up and tapped her on the shoulder. 'I think we should ask a few questions,' he said. 'The doctor she worked for ...'

He grinned. 'Never did trust the medical profession,' he said.

'The trouble is,' she said, 'we haven't really found anything suspicious, have we? We just can't find a cause of death. That's all.'

He picked up her notebook. 'And what about the missing Mr Shiers?'

'We'll get a couple of the blokes to ask around,' she said. 'Maybe he did run off with another woman.'

'Maybe he didn't,' he said. 'Maybe the two things are connected.' He pulled the pad towards him and drew a picture of two houses – crude pictures, like a child's.

'I know this sounds a bit far fetched,' he said. 'But what if ... Look. House one – man disappears. House two. We know Marilyn had a nasty streak in her – wasn't above manipulation – dirty tricks. What if she knew something?'

She was tempted to laugh. It sounded melodramatic – detective novel stuff. But Mike's dark eyes were deadly serious and he was staring at her.

'How?'

He shrugged his shoulders. 'Poison,' he said. 'It was poison.'

'So why hasn't Matthew found it?'

Again Mike's eyes were fixed on her. 'Do a bit of digging,' he said. 'Digging. I reckon Dr Levin knows a bit more about our friend than he's letting on.'

She let out the breath she had been holding and knew this was what had lain at the back of her mind all day.

There were questions she knew she should ask but was frightened to. She didn't really want the answers. But she had gained the distinct impression that Matthew had wanted her to drop the case. Why?

'Matthew's ringing me later on,' she said. She stood up. 'I'm going to call in at the surgery,' she said. 'I want to speak to Dr Wilson again.'

He was sitting in his room, staring out of the window, his face lined and grey, when the receptionist showed her in. He stood up courteously.

'When will this nightmare end?'

'I'm sorry.' She sat down. 'Sudden death – as I'm sure you understand – is never pleasant. There are often unanswered questions. Sometimes we never get the answer, Dr Wilson. But apart from having failed to discover the actual cause of death there are certain anomalies in this case.'

He looked wearily at her. 'It isn't always possible to discover the cause of death,' he said.

She nodded. 'We know that, Doctor. But Marilyn was dressed in a ... suggestive costume. We simply want to make sure.'

His voice cracked. 'You haven't got a perverted rapist on the loose.'

'She wasn't raped,' Joanna said quietly.

The doctor ran his fingers through his greying hair. It was sticking up like a cartoon character's. 'Then why?' he said. 'She wasn't robbed, was she?'

'We don't even know how they got in,' she said.

He suddenly frowned. 'Anomalies?' he queried.

'More money than she should have had ...'

'Her mother ...'

'We're going to check it out.'

She crossed her legs. 'Now I just want to ask a few routine questions. Do you cover all your own nights, Doctor?'

He gave a tired smile. 'God – no,' he said. 'I join up

79

with Sammy Bose's practice by night. There are four of them,' he added, 'so it works out quite well. A one in five rota.'

Something jerked in Joanna's mind. 'Does that mean,' she asked slowly, 'that on the nights you were on call you were Marilyn's doctor too?'

He laughed. 'I suppose I was,' he said. 'I never thought about it. I suppose I was,' he said slowly. 'She never called me . . .'

'And you were on call the night she died?'

Jonah Wilson looked uneasy. 'Now hang on, Inspector,' he said. 'If you're suggesting—'

'I'm not suggesting anything,' she said. 'I'm merely trying to gather facts.'

'Well yes, then – I was.'

'Was it a busy night?'

'A few calls.' His tone had changed. He was no longer the friendly doctor, employer of a dead woman. He was a suspect, rattled and defensive. 'I've told you. I had to go out to Onecote.'

'At what time?' Joanna was writing in her book.

'About eleven . . .' He gave the address. 'I was gone about three-quarters of an hour. She thought she had meningitis.'

'Ah yes, I remember. And it was a false alarm.'

'Yes. A bloody headache.'

Joanna made a mental note to follow it up.

She found the receptionists drinking coffee in the square room where the notes were kept. The room went quiet the instant she walked in. But when they offered her a cup she accepted and they began to relax. She looked at them curiously. 'What was she like?' she asked.

The tall redhead, Sally, took down a photograph pinned to the noticeboard. 'This was Marilyn,' she said.

There were four people in the picture: the two receptionists standing stiffly in paper hats, glasses in their hands. A plump woman, heavily made up, was draped around Dr Wilson. And even though the quality of the picture was poor Joanna could see that the doctor was as uneasy about the situation as Marilyn Smith was relishing it. Joanna looked closer.

There was a lascivious smile on the woman's face. Glossy lipstick, frizzled hair and her mouth slightly open. She was wearing a very short, tight black dress, which revealed inches of deep cleavage and rolls of fat around the waist. Red fingernails hung down the doctor's tweed jacket. Marilyn was looking at him. He was staring unhappily into the camera.

Sally looked over Joanna's shoulder. 'God,' she said quietly. 'If ever a woman had an obscene passion for a man, she did. Worshipped him. Made every sort of play she could. Gave the poor doctor no peace. No peace at all.'

'Did he enjoy the attention?' Joanna said, concealing her surprise.

Sally looked back at the photograph. 'What do you think?' she asked. 'He found her repulsive. He was married. Mrs Wilson may have her problems, but they were a happy couple. He couldn't wait to get home to her at night. He had no time for Marilyn.'

'He must have found it difficult,' she said. 'Embarrassing.'

Maureen nodded. 'He would squirm sometimes.'

'But he kept her on as his nurse.'

Sally grimaced.

'May I borrow this photograph?'

Maureen shrugged her shoulders. 'Have it,' she said. 'We don't want it back.' At Joanna's look of surprise she said aggressively, 'Look – we don't want to be reminded of her. We couldn't stand her.'

'We don't want to speak ill of the dead,' the other said, 'but this place will be happier without her. She manufactured trouble. Always told you the nasty things people might have said about you. Always made life difficult. Some people,' she said, 'won't be missed.' She glanced back at the photograph. 'She's one of them.'

At this moment Jonah wandered through, saw her and hesitated, as though unsure whether to enter or leave.

Joanna pocketed the picture. 'Tell me, Dr Wilson,' she said, 'what's your private opinion? What do you think she died of?'

He looked around nervously. 'Well, as I've already told you, I don't think she really was the type to commit suicide,' he said slowly. 'Although you never can tell. Most suicides have made one attempt before. But then people do sometimes bottle things up.' He frowned. 'Maybe some sort of accident?' He gave a shy smile.

It was an unsatisfactory answer and Joanna felt irritated. Damn it, she thought. She was the investigating officer. It was up to her to decide. Murder investigations were expensive. Suicides cheap. And all this flamming from the medical profession was making it bloody hard to decide which this case was. All the time she was busy here she was missing from somewhere else.

'Boyfriend?' she said.

'No one ever came here,' the doctor said calmly.

She was going to get no help from here, she decided, and left.

Matthew rang her almost as soon as she arrived back at the station. His voice sounded tight and strained. 'Are you busy?' he asked curtly.

She replied yes and then he asked her if she had time to talk. Again she said yes.

'I can't let go of you, Jo,' he said. 'I can't stop thinking about you.'

She felt her heart pounding against her chest and wished he had not rung.

'Are you there?' he asked, in the same, strangled voice.

'Matthew,' she said softly. 'Give it some time – please.'

He sighed. 'I can't, Jo. I've tried.'

'For God's sake, Matthew,' she said, suddenly irritated. 'You're married. You have a daughter. You want to stay that way. That's fine by me but don't involve me on the sidelines. Work your life out . . .'

'Don't you know what I'm saying, Jo? I love you.'

She felt herself shake with a sudden strong anger. 'I don't want to go through it all again, Matthew,' she said. 'All the waiting and hoping. Please – leave me to get on with my life. I have work to do.'

He paused. 'How's it going?'

She answered not well.

'Did the SOCOs find anything?'

She had always loved the way he lapsed into police jargon, although it felt dangerously familiar to be discussing cases with him.

'They've found bugger all,' she said. 'Alsatian hairs, her fingerprints. Little else. It's almost unnatural. The woman led the life of a nun.'

Matthew gave a strained laugh. 'She didn't look like that to me. That was no nun lying there on the slab.'

'She wasn't dressed like a nun,' Joanna agreed, 'but there's no sign of riotous living in the house in Silk Street. What about you? Have you got the results from the path lab?'

'Some. There'll be more coming through over the next few days. The stomach contents revealed tiny traces of barbiturates which would have made her sleepy but certainly not killed her. Alcohol . . . I think . . .' He paused. 'This is just a theory, but I think she might have used the champagne as an aphrodisiac. I've sent the viscera and more samples off to the forensic lab in Birmingham but you know how long that can take. Do you know what I wish?' he asked, and without waiting for a comment said, 'I wish I could put on the death certificate that she just died. Cause unknown . . .'

Joanna was puzzled by his attitude. He was a pathologist. 'Matthew,' she remonstrated. 'How can you say that? Surely you want to find out? Healthy women in their late thirties don't just die.'

'But it would fit in neatly, wouldn't it?' he asked. 'The

dog ... no sign of a break-in. No forced entry. Nothing broken, damaged or stolen from the house. You have to face it, Jo,' he said, 'it's the only explanation that fits in with everything – including the fact that I can't find a mark on the body.'

Privately she knew she had to agree with him.

There was a pause from the other end, then Matthew said, 'So what about us?'

She was silent. Then, after endless seconds, she said, 'Matthew. Ring me when you have more results, please. I have to go now,' and she hung up.

She was left staring at the phone with a vague feeling of disquiet. Had she ever really known him? Small voices whispered the answer to her. No ... Matthew Levin was a stranger.

She was about to leave the station for the evening when the duty sergeant called her.

'Telephone,' he said, then made a face. 'Nutter ...'

She picked it up. 'I want to speak to' – there was a pause – 'Detective Inspector Piercy.'

She recognized the wavering voice immediately. 'Good evening, Mrs Shiers,' she said. 'It's DI Piercy here. What can I do for you?'

There was a sharp intake of breath, then the words came tumbling out. 'I'm so frightened ... Please send someone round here.'

'What's the matter, Mrs Shiers?'

'Please ...' The voice sobbed. 'Please send someone round. I heard the dog,' she said. 'I heard Ben ...'

In spite of common sense telling her this was impossible, Joanna felt herself grow quite cold. Ben was dead. She tried to tell Evelyn Shiers. The dog had gone to the vet's. He had been put to sleep.

Evelyn was most insistent. 'I heard him,' she said. 'Do you think I could have imagined it? I heard the dog.'

The duty sergeant looked at Joanna enquiringly.

She tried to make light of it. 'Ghost dog,' she said apologetically. 'Better get a squad car round.'

The duty sergeant chuckled and picked up the phone. He was going to enjoy telling this to his mates in the pub.

Joanna picked up her bag. 'Ring me at home,' she said. 'I'll be back in an hour.'

# Chapter 9

She was about to run a bath when the phone rang.

'There wasn't a dog there. The place was deserted.'

'No barking?'

'It was quiet.' The constable was speaking from his car phone. She could hear the crackle. 'We looked all over – spent half an hour there. Nothing doing. No dog.'

Joanna frowned. 'And how was Mrs Shiers?'

'Bloody hysterical,' the constable said. 'Doing her nut. We tried to convince her but she wasn't having it. She was sure the dog was still inside.'

The vague feeling of disquiet refused to go. 'And the house?'

'Deserted,' he said. 'No one there. We had a good look round. Nothing. Not another dead body or another fierce dog.'

'What did Mrs Shiers say?' Joanna asked.

'She insisted it was Ben.' He sounded sceptical. 'Said she knew his bark.'

Joanna heard an explosion of laughter in the squad car. 'OK,' she said. 'Thanks.' She replaced the phone, wondering whether it was possible to recognize a dog by its bark.

The question seeped into her dreams that night and by morning she still didn't know the answer.

The house was still today – so still she knew it was filled with diaphanous memories. She wandered from room to room.

'Stevie,' she whispered. 'Stevie . . . Are you there?'

She wandered into the kitchen to collect the baby's bottle but Jonah must have hidden it again. She searched for it, pulled things out of drawers . . . tea towels and hand towels . . . spoons and plates. Saucepans and packets of cereal. Where was it?

She walked through to the living room and smiled. Jonah liked it tidy . . . all the toys put away. That was how Jonah liked it. Then up the stairs to run the child's bath.

She heard the chuckling as she reached the halfway step. It was always like this. She could hear Stevie. But then naughty Stevie would hide when she reached the top step. He sometimes hid in the nursery, so when she reached the top of the stairs that was where she headed. But when she reached the door with a pink rabbit on it she stopped, reached out to turn the handle, already knowing that it would be locked . . .

It didn't improve Joanna's mood that morning to have her leg pulled. 'Heard the one about the phantom dog, Inspector?'

She waited by the desk. 'Tell me,' she said.

'Bit the bugger on the bum.' The duty sergeant exploded into giggles, joined by the two lads from traffic. She gave a quick smile.

'By the way,' he said. 'She's rung again.'

She raised her eyebrows. 'Same thing, Martin?'

He nodded. 'Getting to be a right pest, this phantom dog.'

The telephone rang and he jerked his thumb towards it. 'That'll be her now,' he said. 'Nine o'clock prompt.'

'I'll take it in my room.'

The voice on the other end sounded hysterical. 'I know it's Ben,' she sobbed. 'I know the sound of his bark.'

'Do you have someone who can come and stay with you?'

'I don't need someone. Just do something. Stop him barking. Please . . . I know it's Ben.'

'Mrs Shiers,' Joanna said soothingly. 'Ben was put down. The vet couldn't cope with him. He put him to sleep. Marilyn wanted it that way. She left instructions.'

'Inspector . . .' Evelyn's voice was panic-struck now. 'Inspector . . . I know it was Ben. I have lived next door to him for two years. I know the sound of his bark almost as well as the sound of my own voice. It was Ben.'

Joanna promised to look into it and replaced the phone, then picked it up straight away. Roderick Beeston was on the line in a matter of seconds.

'I know this probably sounds a silly question, Mr Beeston,' she said cautiously, 'but there is no doubt about it, is there? It was Ben you put down – wasn't it?'

'What's all this about?' His voice was deep and suspicious.

Even to her the whole thing sounded illogical. She stalled for a moment. 'Tell me, Mr Beeston,' she said. 'Is it possible to distinguish the sound of one dog from another?'

'You mean – do dogs have individual barks?' He paused. 'That's a good question, Inspector. Not one I would have expected the police to be interested in.'

'I'm interested in anything that might have a bearing on this case,' she said crisply.

'Well now, I'm intrigued. The answer is – I believe so,' he said, 'provided you know the dog well enough. I think you can.'

She was silent for a moment then said quickly, 'Marilyn Smith's next door neighbour has rung us six times in the last twenty-four hours, convinced she has heard Ben barking.'

Roderick Beeston cleared his throat. 'Now that is interesting,' he said.

'So I thought I'd check with you.'

'There's no doubt about it,' the vet said. 'Ben's dead. I scattered the ashes myself. On the roses, as it happens.'

Joanna felt slightly sick. She thanked the vet and sat twiddling her pencil. As soon as she heard Mike's voice outside she called him in.

'I thought we were going to Cardiff today,' he said. 'I told my wife.'

She ignored his irritation and told him about the phantom dog. 'What do you make of it?'

'I'll tell you what I make of it,' he said. 'Guilty conscience.' He stared at her. 'She's having nightmares because she knows something we don't. Now, are we going to Cardiff?'

'This afternoon,' she said. 'I want to go back to the surgery. I want to find out a few more things about Marilyn. Mike.' She suddenly stopped. 'Do you think it's possible Marilyn was blackmailing Evelyn Shiers over something to do with the disappearance of her husband?'

'Maybe,' he said. 'But I can't see her killing her husband.'

'Perhaps,' she said, 'it wasn't a killing. Maybe it was something else. Maybe, we should dig up the garden.'

They put Constable Willis on the job to ask questions at the engineering company where Jock Shiers had worked until four years earlier.

The foreman was a stout man with acne scarring. 'I remember Jock,' he said. 'Good man – regular as clockwork. Jet black hair.' He frowned. 'Passion for sailing.'

'Really?' PC Willis raised his eyebrows.

'Yes.' The foreman grinned. 'Had a boat called the *Marie Celeste*. Always thought it an unfortunate name myself but Jock had quite a sense of humour.'

'You must have thought it strange when he didn't turn up for work.'

The foreman sighed. 'Well,' he said slowly. 'I did and I didn't. He was a strange, unpredictable character. Often did weird things. So when Mrs Shiers said he'd decided to take off in that boat of his I wasn't really that surprised – not really.' He gave the PC a quick, curious look. 'What's happened? Something funny going on?'

'We're just making enquiries,' Willis said.

The foreman gave a sceptical chuckle. 'I've heard that one before as well,' he said. 'Don't give me that. You're wondering what's happened to old Jock, aren't you?' He scratched his head then gave a sudden exclamation of enlightenment. 'Of course!' he said. 'That dead nurse. Lived next door to them, didn't she? Well, surely Mrs Shiers can tell you where Jock is, can't she?'

Willis picked up his helmet and the foreman followed him out. 'Come on,' he said. 'You can tell me. What are you thinking?'

'Just routine enquiries,' Willis said, letting himself into the car. He drove off, leaving the foreman staring after him.

Joanna sat patiently in the waiting room for the doctor to finish his surgery at eleven. There were still a few patients to be seen; Dr Wilson's buzzer was busy, summoning the sick. Marilyn Smith's buzzer was silent.

At last the waiting room was empty and the receptionist called her through. 'He'll see you now.'

She could tell from the receptionists' hostile eyes that they were asking questions. Why hadn't she tracked down the reason for Marilyn's death? Why hadn't she caught the killer – if there was a killer? Why was she still asking questions – and giving no answers? Why was everything taking so long? Even Dr Wilson looked irritated by yet another visit from the police.

'What now?' he said, then seemed to regret his abruptness. 'Sorry. It can be difficult being a GP in a small town. It's tricky dining with people one night and the next day peering into their insides. Besides . . .' He blinked. 'Secrecy . . .' He looked at her then with bright, shining eyes. 'Secrecy,' he said again. 'It's so important. Secrecy must be preserved at all costs.'

Joanna felt uncomfortable but she nodded.

'You know . . . it's only now – since she died – that I realize. I hardly knew Marilyn at all.' The doctor was watching her face very carefully. 'Although we worked together – met every day for the past few years – I didn't really know her. You see,' he added, 'we only really met at work.' He reinforced this point a little too emphatically for her liking.

Was it the nasty, suspicious police mind that made her think, 'Doth protest too much'?

'Like I said before, she was good at her job,' the doctor continued.

He dropped his eyes suddenly and Joanna knew he was not being straight with her.

Why? What was the point?

Again she felt uneasy. Of all the people who could best mimic a natural or puzzling death she feared doctors most. They had knowledge. They also had the means. And if Marilyn had been murdered, it had been a carefully concealed act.

'Was she very fond of her mother?' she asked. 'Unduly upset at her death?'

'Not particularly,' the doctor said. 'She had some time off for the funeral and to dispose of the house and things.' He thought for a moment. 'No,' he said finally. 'I can't say she seemed very upset.'

'Was she depressed lately?'

He shook his head. 'No – she wasn't.'

She looked at him again and smiled encouragingly. 'What sort of a person was she? What did she look like? Was she pretty?'

The doctor looked at her. 'Inspector,' he said patiently. 'You've seen the photograph. I wasn't having an affair with my nurse. Why do you people have to be so suspicious?'

'It's my job,' she said shortly. 'And I'm fumbling in the dark, Doctor. I'm heading out in all sorts of directions . . . working blind. And until I have a cause of death I can't drop the case or direct my investigations towards something more relevant.'

He met her eyes. 'I sympathize, Inspector,' he said, and she found herself thinking – as had no doubt countless previous patients – what lovely eyes he had, direct and fearless, honest but tired. He looked as though his life had been trying.

'You never knew Marilyn alive, did you?' he asked.

She shook her head. 'No.'

He stopped for a minute, then said quietly, 'If you had known her you would realize. Nothing – nothing that ever happened to her was inexplicable.'

Joanna stared at him, puzzled. Taking advantage of the pause in questioning, Dr Wilson muttered something about house calls, stood up and left the room.

She decided to tackle the receptionists again. They needed little encouragement.

'All this fuss,' said Sally venomously. 'You know, she would have loved it – revelled in it. I wouldn't be a bit surprised if she planned the whole damned thing.'

'It's possible,' Joanna said cautiously.

Sally tossed her head in disgust. 'Honestly,' she said.

'You said she didn't have a boyfriend. Did anyone ever come to see her here? Friends?'

It was Maureen who answered. She shrugged her shoulders. 'No,' she said. 'I never met any. No one ever came here for her except patients.'

Joanna frowned. Except patients ...

'Which patients came regularly?' she asked.

The receptionists glanced quickly at one another. 'Lots of them ... diabetics and asthmatics, anyone with chronic disease.'

She bit her lip, leaned forwards in her chair. 'Anyone who didn't have a chronic disease?' she asked.

'Well ...' Sally was floundering.

It was Maureen who came to her rescue. 'One or two,' she said.

'Who?'

'A few people we did wonder about,' the receptionist said. 'The undertaker was one of them.'

'Do you mean Paul Haddon?'

'Every month,' Sally confirmed. 'First Thursday in the month.'

'Very angry he was sometimes.'

'Angry?'

The receptionist glanced through the hatch into the patients' waiting room. 'He'd pace up and down there in a fury, getting redder and redder.

'You want to watch it, Mr Haddon,' I said. 'You'll make your blood pressure worse.'

She paused. 'Swore at me, he did. Nothing wrong with my effing blood pressure. Cheeky thing.'

'Well, perhaps he had another illness?'

'When Smithy came out I asked her. What's wrong with that undertaker . . .? She was that haughty when she answered. Blood pressure . . . What I say is, Inspector – one of them was lying.'

Joanna made a mental note to speak to the undertaker. 'Anyone else?'

The two women looked at each other. 'I don't think there was much up with that antique dealer.'

Joanna pricked up her ears. 'Was he a frequent visitor?'

'Few times a year . . .'

'And in the same bad temper,' Maureen added. 'There was more to those visits than met the eye.'

Sally looked at Joanna. 'Who's had Ben?' she asked. 'I can't imagine him with anyone but Marilyn. She wouldn't even have a holiday abroad because of Ben.'

'I'm afraid Ben's had to be put down,' Joanna said.

Both women nodded regretfully.

'She would have wanted that,' Sally averred. 'She told me once that if she died she wanted Ben put down. I thought it was a shame – told her so.'

'What did she say?' Joanna asked curiously.

'Gave a little laugh and one of those superior smiles of hers. "Ben would rather be dead than live without me",' Sally mimicked.

'Ben had no bloody choice,' Maureen said bitterly. 'Sadistic cow.'

And this gave another ugly twist to the dead woman's character. If denied life herself she wanted her beloved pet to share death.

'And you're sure you can't recall her talking about any relatives?' Joanna pressed.

'She told us she was the last of a long line.' Maureen dropped her chin on to her chest in a sceptical glance. 'Believe that if you want. There was no touch of class about her. She just liked to pretend. Long line ...' She grimaced. 'Long line of whores.'

Joanna's mind was cast back involuntarily to the pink-tinged bedroom ... splayed legs ... Make-believe had played a large part in the dead woman's life. The trouble was sorting out the truth from the lies. Somewhere in a haze of pink chiffon and cheap scent was a fact. Marilyn Smith was dead. Perhaps the visit to her origins this afternoon would be enlightening.

'Do you know where she came from?'

'Yes, I think it was Cardiff.' Sally was frowning in concentration. 'I'm sure she said it was Cardiff.'

That – at least – was right.

'She definitely wasn't a local girl.'

'I thought I could hear that bit of Welsh in her voice. Didn't you think so, Maureen?'

Maureen nodded vaguely. 'Perhaps,' she said.

Joanna frowned. 'What exactly did she say to you about her affair with a married man? Was it true?'

'Who knows ...?' Sally's eyes met hers. 'Who knew with Marilyn what was the truth and what was a pack of lies?'

'Sometimes,' Maureen said quietly, 'I don't think even she knew what was the truth and what was lies. I think she deceived herself so bloody completely she started to believe her own stories.'

And the underwear, Joanna thought. An extension to the self-deception? She glanced from one woman to the other.

'Can you tell me,' she asked tentatively, 'any more about relations between Dr Wilson and Marilyn? You told me before that she gave him no peace. Why didn't he ask her to leave?'

The two women looked at one another.

'I'd see him *look* at her sometimes as though he could have given her her cards, but . . .'

'He wouldn't dare.' Maureen's face was round and incredulous. 'His wife wouldn't have let him.'

'Mrs Wilson?' Joanna said. 'What's she got to do with it?'

'It was through her that Marilyn Smith got the job.'

Joanna pricked up her ears. 'Do go on,' she said softly.

'Mrs Wilson left years ago to have the baby,' Sally explained. 'It was all ever so sad. She used to be the nurse here. It worked very well. She and Dr Wilson always got on like a house on fire. And she was a wonderful nurse – ever so kind and sweet. Anyway, she left to have the baby and Marilyn came. They were old friends, you see. They were nurses together in Birmingham, where Dr Wilson trained.'

'Do you mean,' Joanna said slowly, 'that Dr Wilson knew Marilyn before she came to work here?'

'Yes . . .' Sally seemed surprised that Joanna did not know. 'Mrs Wilson and Marilyn were best friends. Didn't you know?'

He had deliberately concealed the fact.

'No,' she said shortly. 'I didn't.' She hadn't known because he hadn't told her. The innocent, hard-working doctor was not quite all he had pretended to be.

'And how many children do they have now?' she asked, more to conceal her irritation than for any other reason. But the effect was dramatic.

The receptionists looked at one another again. Sally was pale. Maureen drew in a sharp intake of breath. Her eyes filled with tears. She scrabbled in her pocket for a handkerchief, found one, dabbed her eyes and looked at Joanna. 'I'm sorry,' she said. 'It was a few years ago but I still feel awful when I remember.'

Joanna could only watch. 'Children?' she prompted delicately.

'It died.' Maureen's face looked stricken. 'Just a few

months old and he died.' She sniffed loudly.

'And Mrs Wilson didn't return to work?'

The reaction surprised her. The redhead's eyes glittered. 'That poor woman,' she said fiercely. 'She's got nothing to do with this. Nothing at all. You just leave her out of it.'

Joanna made a mental note to do nothing of the sort.

'She's been ill ever since the baby died,' Maureen continued reluctantly. 'She doesn't go out of the house. The doctor does all the shopping as well as working here. He does everything for her – even buys her clothes. I've seen him,' she said defensively as Sally gave her a sharp look, 'in Marks and Spencer.'

Joanna stood up to leave. 'Thank you,' she said, 'you've been a real help.'


'Where the bloody hell have you been?'

Mike was in a rage when she finally arrived back at the station. 'I thought we were going to Cardiff.'

'Tomorrow,' she said.

He looked disgruntled.

'I told my old lady we were off there today.'

She shrugged. 'What's the difference? Anyway,' she sat down, 'I've been to the surgery and found out some rather interesting facts . . .' Quickly she filled him in.

He still looked sour. 'Puts the doctor in a slightly different light, doesn't it?'

She was forced to agree.

'Hardly bloody Albert Schweitzer, is he?'

'Even doctors are human,' she said.

He gave an ugly smile. 'Aren't they just?' he said.

She ignored his comment. 'Get back to the facts, Mike,' she said. 'If everyone says Marilyn's mother died four or five years ago and that's where all the money came from, who the hell is writing her letters signing them love Mum, and where the heck did all the money come from?' She gave a deep sigh. 'The trouble with this case is, yes, there are lots of lies. But there are facts, too. There was a lot of money. It did come from somewhere. The blasted woman is dead. But practically everything else is fog, lies and . . .' She ran her fingers through her hair and cupped her chin in her hand. 'So where are we, Mike?' she said slowly. 'Do you smell blackmail?'

'Maybe,' he said cautiously.

'And what can follow from blackmail?'

He scowled. 'We've no evidence of murder.'

She pointed her finger at him. 'That's what worries me,' she said. 'Evidence. How many times have you and I known a truth and had no evidence? It doesn't take the truth away – it simply makes it impossible to prove in a court of law.'

He stared at her, his shoulders rigid, then slowly he nodded. 'You're right,' he said simply. 'You're right.'

'So,' she said, 'now you know why I'm not dropping the case.'

'Right,' he said again.

He pulled up a chair and flipped a report across the desk. 'You'll want to read these,' he said. 'The forensic report on the bedding they took away and some more results from the path lab.'

'Thanks, Mike.'

He stood up. 'Want a coffee?' He spoke casually. It fooled neither of them and she knew the effort had cost him. He was not a natural tea boy.

'Thank you,' she said again.

Bedding . . . Her eyes scanned quickly down the sheet, picking out points of interest. No semen . . . Hair found, dark brown, some grey, various dyes and rinses, permed around four months ago.

Her thoughts went back to the Christmas photograph on the noticeboard in the doctor's reception area. Christmas – recently permed. She glanced again at the report. Other hair found, pubic hair, similar to the sample taken from the body.

She looked at the second page. Fibres – natural cotton, polyester . . . similar to samples . . . silk and some black nylon . . . It all matched.

Mike returned with the coffee and slid a sachet of

sugar and another of dried milk across the desk to her.

'Didn't know whether you took it,' he said grumpily, and she knew comments had been made at the coffee machine. Sucking up to your boss... Demoted to tea boy? She could well imagine it.

He perched on the edge of the desk and drank his coffee. 'There isn't a single sample that doesn't match items in her wardrobe,' he said. 'And the report on the stomach contents revealed what we thought: a meal of steak, chips, salad.' He bit his lip. 'There was one thing, though – there was a capsule ... partially digested.'

Joanna felt depressed. 'Her sleeping tablets, Mike. They were capsules.'

He nodded. 'I thought they might be.' He leaned across, picked up the phone. 'I'd better ring them, let them know we found sleeping tablets in the bedroom.'

She picked up the page headed Stomach Contents and one phrase leapt out at her. 'Red and yellow,' she said quickly. 'The capsules we found by the bed were black and green.'

'That's strange.' Mike frowned. 'Are you sure?'

She nodded.

'But they didn't find any lethal blood levels,' he mused. 'Small amounts of barbiturate – that's all – that and some champagne. And why take barbiturates if you're waiting for a lover?' His dark eyes fixed on hers. 'I would have thought it would be the last thing you'd want – to fall asleep.'

'But it's something,' Joanna said slowly. 'Something unusual – something that didn't belong in the house. It's the very first thing.' She looked at him. 'You know how these things develop, Mike. Get the SOCOs to look through their records for a bottle of capsules red and yellow.'

It was late by the time they had finished writing reports and Joanna knew it was Mike's night at the gym. So it was tentatively that she asked him to call in at the funeral parlour with her on the way home.

'Please,' she said. 'I won't take very long. I only want to ask him a couple of things.'

He looked grumpily at her. 'Are we going to interview every single bloody patient?' he asked.

'No – not all.'

'So what's so special about him?'

She picked up her jacket. 'I almost daren't use the word "feeling".'

'It's only because he's an undertaker – wears black, connected with death.'

'No, Mike,' she said. 'He called in to see her regularly, for no obvious reason. I have to know. What was she blackmailing him about?'

He left still unconvinced.


The chapel of rest was panelled in light oak, a small altar at one end, flowers on a tall pedestal, four rows of plush-covered chairs.

Joanna watched the undertaker curiously. 'How well did you know Marilyn?' She purposely used the nurse's Christian name to familiarize the relationship, but Paul Haddon merely blinked.

'You mean Sister Smith?'

'Yes.' She let her voice linger with implication.

'Hardly at all.'

His jacket strained over a small pot belly, fastened by only one of four buttons. 'I was just one of her patients,' he said. 'I didn't know her – not personally.'

'What did you attend for, so regularly?'

He blustered. 'That's a professional secret.'

He had an unattractive mouth, Joanna thought. Slack and moist; the lower lip hung down as he talked.

'In a murder trial there aren't any secrets – professional or otherwise, Mr Haddon,' she said. Joanna was glad Mike was with her. The undertaker's pale face and dark, unreadable eyes were making her feel uncomfortable in this cold, uneasy place.

'I have high blood pressure. I had to see her every month.'

Joanna nodded. 'You had to see her, Mr Haddon, but it was bugger all to do with your blood pressure.'

She decided to go for the full frontal attack. 'What was she blackmailing you about?'

The effect on Paul Haddon was startling. His eyes bulged, his face drained of blood. His Adam's apple bobbed up and down furiously. He opened his mouth to speak. Nothing came out but a strangled sob. He grasped the back of one of the chairs and slumped on to it gratefully.

'No right,' he gasped, when he could speak. 'Not true . . . not true.'

She felt almost sorry for him. 'Did you kill her, Mr Haddon?'

Now he looked terrified. Vigorously he shook his head. 'No . . .' he said. 'No . . . No. Not me.'

'Then who?'

They were the first words Mike had spoken since they had arrived. She had known he was uneasy here. Now she looked at him. His face was set and hard. She didn't need to convince him any more. Marilyn Smith had been murdered. The questions were twofold: how, and by whom?

She turned her attention back to the undertaker.

'I don't know . . .' He was having trouble breathing. 'I don't know.'

'I should go and see a decent doctor if I were you.' Mike's voice was hard and unsympathetic. He didn't look at Joanna.

Paul Haddon gave a feeble smile. It made him seem even more repulsive.

# Chapter 10

Mike was watching her hands on the wheel. 'What on earth are you going to tell her?'

Joanna sighed. 'I know what I'm not going to tell her,' she said, keeping her eyes on the car in front. 'I'm not going to tell her her daughter spun a story that she'd died five years ago.'

She looked at Mike quickly. 'Can you imagine how hurt she would feel?' She sighed again. 'Damn it, Mike, this has to be the shitty end of the job, telling someone that we have no idea how her daughter died. She's bound to feel upset. I'm just glad it wasn't us who had to tell her that Marilyn's dead.' She frowned. 'I feel we're failing.'

Joanna swerved to miss a car that pulled out without indicating.

'Bastard,' Mike muttered.

Joanna smiled and turned her face slightly so Mike missed her amusement. 'Ghosts don't write letters, Mike. Of course she's alive. Ghosts don't bark either,' she said.

He gave her a quick glance. 'Mrs Shiers?'

She nodded. 'She rings up about three times a day. She's driving everyone mad.'

'It's a guilty conscience,' he said.

She looked at him. 'Is it?'

He gave a strangled laugh. 'You don't believe that crap about ghost dogs?'

'No,' she said quickly. 'Of course not.'

'So it's in her mind, isn't it? Guilt about her husband.'

'The *Marie Celeste* was moored off Anglesey,' she said. 'It was there for a few years.'

'Has anybody seen it recently?'

'The local police are investigating.'

'Damn.' Mike swore as a chain of brake lights suddenly flashed on.

Joanna slowed down and just as quickly the traffic speeded up again.

Mike glanced down at the letter. 'So where did the money come from?' He gave her a quick glance. 'Everyone says it was left her by her mother.'

Joanna tucked her hair behind her ears. 'My guess is blackmail . . . We have a long list. Take your choice. Evelyn . . . our friend the undertaker. Then there's your friend – Grenville Machin, the antique dealer. We haven't even begun to investigate him. And Dr Wilson has been less than truthful.'

Mike gave an explosive laugh. 'You're not bloody short of suspects,' he said. 'But we don't know how she died. Your pathologist hasn't come up with anything very clever, has he?'

'He isn't *my* pathologist,' she said crossly. Had she not been driving she would probably have stamped her foot right now. But the truth was she knew she would have to speak to Matthew again. She'd been putting it off.

'Mike . . .' She gave him a swift glance. 'If it is Machin, this case might be your chance to nail him. And you know how thorough these investigations need to be.' She gave him a quick grin. 'We've got an excuse now to look a little deeper into the affairs of our friend. Besides . . .' she said gaily, 'I'm looking forward to meeting him.'

The thought seemed to amuse Mike. He gave a deep chuckle.

'Well,' she said, 'he's the only person involved with Marilyn to have any large amounts of suspect money. Didn't you say he owns that huge house on the Longley Road?'

Mike nodded.

'Well, just think of it, Mike. Think of Marilyn's lifestyle . . . That house, the antiques, the plastic surgery – everything. We're talking about a lot of money here. It has to have come from him.'

'What about the others?'

'No real sign of wealth.' She paused. 'I mean – how much money do you think she could have squeezed out of Evelyn? Not much. Haddon?' She made a face. 'Not a rich man. But our friend Machin . . .' She looked at him excitedly. 'He's already been had up for attempted murder . . .'

Mike grinned. 'Yes,' he said slowly. 'You're getting me quite excited. I'd love that. Nail him for murder.'

But Joanna held up her hand. 'We haven't got evidence of murder yet,' she said, 'let alone proof that he did it. I'm still waiting for further reports from Dr Levin.'

Mike was silent for a moment and she knew exactly where his thoughts were taking him. She gave him a quick glance and he caught her eye. She knew until they had squared this one they had no hope of a trusting working relationship.

Mike cleared his throat. 'You can call him Matthew,' he said. 'I know you know him at least well enough for that.'

She was silent, embarrassed, until he spoke again.

'It hasn't made it any easier, you know – working under a woman and knowing more about her than I ought to.'

'We were lovers. We're not any more. That's all there is to it,' she said simply.

He chewed his lip. 'I don't expect his wife feels like that. My wife doesn't like it much either – having it off with married men.'

She felt herself flush. Caught out. 'Well he's still with his wife,' she said bitterly. 'So it hasn't done them that much harm.'

'How do you know?'

It was Mike who changed the subject. 'You're sure the uniformed men have already told her?'

She nodded. 'Yes, and warned her we would be along today.'

She was silent again and after a few minutes he spoke again.

'Are you convinced Marilyn was killed?'

She nodded. 'Even more than I was.'

'On the strength of one capsule?'

'That may be all we've found so far. There's more, I'm sure of it. There are too many unanswered questions, Mike. And even when I get satisfactory answers or Matthew discovers a good big blood clot somewhere I'll still be suspicious. I don't think I'll believe she died alone, in bed, of natural causes even if they find something *really* convincing. Mike, I believe she was blackmailing someone – possibly more than one person, and we both know who one of them probably was. In fact,' she said, 'once we've spoken to Mrs Smith I quite look forward to meeting your Mr Machin. But I don't think we're anywhere near the truth about this case. I think she was murdered quite cleverly by someone who had knowledge and access to her home.'

'And what about the dog?'

'If Marilyn let the person in he might have accepted him – or her.'

'But that's pretty unlikely, from what we know of Ben. Not even a bark? What about the stuff the vet had?' Mike asked.

She shook her head. 'It's on a small trial,' she said. 'There are only a couple of vets in the country trying it out. And all the canisters are accounted for. It's better guarded than heroin. Besides ... he did a post-mortem on Ben. He wasn't drugged, Mike.'

She sighed. 'Sordid things, aren't they, murders? Always accidents and small reasons. Always the same ones – money, sex, revenge – same old merry-go-round. Roll up, take your pick. Mix them up a little, shake them, but it's always the same few reasons.'

He glanced at her. 'I do believe, madam,' he said formally, 'that your promotion has made you cynical.'

'Mike!' She almost exploded. 'When we're alone call me Joanna – please. We're going to have to work together, probably for several years, in difficult and close circumstances. You already know my innermost secrets – ones I bloody well wish you didn't know. For God's sake, call me Joanna.'

He half smiled. 'OK, then, Joanna.'

She guided the car towards the M5 turn-off, then settled down comfortably at seventy miles an hour.

A car cut in front of them from the outside lane and she pointed. 'Look at that for rotten driving.'

Mike grimaced. 'Woman driver,' he grunted.

She cast him a look. 'What happened to new man, Mike?' she asked suddenly. 'To the abolition of sexual discrimination inside the police force? Why can't you just accept the opposite sex? What's so damned different about us?'

'I do accept you,' he protested, and she smiled. His bull neck was fierce red.

They were quiet for the next few miles but she could sense Mike was building up to say something. He shifted uncomfortably in his seat. He was debating whether to risk it. Eventually he did.

'I'll tell you something,' he paused, 'Joanna. I'll tell you why I object to women in the police force. They aren't equal – that's why. When you get a flat tyre it's the bloody men who come and change the wheel. When you have to go out on a call you never send a woman police officer on her own. Rape victims, women – have to have a woman officer. Violent situations – always spare the woman. We have to mollycoddle you, make allowances all the time for your sex. That makes me angry. I have nothing against you personally. In fact, if you want to know the truth I quite like you. For what you are I think you've your head screwed on. But I think women want it all ways. They even,' he carried on angrily, rising to his subject, 'want a special MP now for women's rights. What about men's rights? – that's what I want to know. Positive discrimination – that's what it is, Joanna. That's what men are suffering these days. We don't know where we are any more.'

She took in a deep breath. 'I quite agree,' she said calmly.

He stopped in his tracks. 'You do?'

'Yes,' she said, 'I do. You're right, Mike. Things have tipped too far. Men are confused, but I'm not personally responsible. Women have had the vote for less than a hundred years. Give us time. Let us settle down. We've not long left the kitchen sink behind. We're still adjusting. Don't be hard on us. In a few years we won't need to be either strident and masculine or bimbos. We'll be well-adjusted citizens.' She grinned at him, glad he had voiced his prejudices. 'Until then, Mike, let's work together and I will try not to use my sex to manipulate you. And you don't resent me – or my sex – if we get it wrong sometimes? All right?'

The policeman smiled and for the first time she felt the warmth of friendship towards him.

'All right,' he said, 'but don't expect me to make allowances. Mind you,' he warned, 'if I see your standards slipping ...'

'You'll be the first to throw bricks at me,' she finished. 'Now is that all?'

'There is something else,' he said unhappily, 'that you haven't touched on. We police work odd hours – day and night. My wife – God bless her – is a jealous woman. She's not too happy about me gallivanting all over the place with you either. You have to understand it's another objection. She'd far rather me be with a bloke.'

Joanna sighed. 'That I can't do anything about,' she said. 'Male prejudices are easy. Female ones impossible to deal with. But I'd be very unhappy about you being taken off the case.' She swung the wheel to leave the motorway and join the M50. 'Hell,' she said, 'I'm only just getting used to you.'

They were quiet from then on all the way into Cardiff,

but it was a companionable silence. As they left the motorway and approached the centre of Cardiff Mike pulled out an A–Z of the city and Joanna manoeuvred the car along busy roads to an endless row of neat terraced houses.

They were tall, three storeys high, each with its own gable window and a tiny pocket handkerchief garden entered by a small wrought iron gate. She pulled into a space in the long line of cars and together they took the three steps between a row of tubbed shrubs to the door. Mike knocked.

A curtain in the bay window was flicked open and they found themselves staring at a pair of unfriendly dark eyes.

Joanna smiled encouragingly and held up her ID card. 'Police,' she mouthed. She turned to Mike. 'Back to the charm school,' she said.

Through ribbed glass the furred shape of a woman approached the front door and it was tugged. But the damp made it stick and it needed a shove from Mike to swing it wide.

The woman stood blocking it. 'Yes?' she said suspiciously, glancing up and down the street. 'Has there been another break-in?'

'No.' Joanna drew a deep breath. This was not going to be easy. 'You are Mrs Smith?'

'Yes,' the woman said, 'I am.'

Joanna stepped forward. 'The mother of Marilyn Smith?' she asked.

The woman glared at them. 'Yes. I suppose you're the detectives from Staffordshire they told me about.'

'That's right.'

So – one question at least answered. Marilyn's mother was definitely alive and well. But Mrs Smith's next response took her aback.

'Who has to pay for the funeral?' she snapped. 'I'm not a wealthy woman. I only have my pension to live on. And Marilyn won't be sending me no more money now, will she?'

Joanna muttered something, shocked, and glanced at

Mike. His face was wooden, his eyes carefully averted.

'Well, come in, come in,' the woman said sharply. 'It doesn't do me any good having police here. People will wonder.'

She glared at Joanna. 'People will talk,' she said, pressing her lips together. 'Where are you parked? Not right outside, I hope.' She leaned her head to one side. 'And I bet you're in a marked car.'

Joanna reassured her. 'We never travel in marked cars,' she said. 'We're CID.'

'Same difference. I don't want the neighbours thinking...' She peered at them. 'And they're quick to think round here.'

'We're parked a little up the road.' Already Joanna felt a profound dislike for this woman. Once inside she wasted no time. 'I'm afraid we still don't know how your daughter died,' she began. 'The pathologist will be carrying out some more tests. Until we know her cause of death we cannot release the body for burial. They'll be holding an inquest just as soon as we've gathered all the facts.'

Marilyn's mother looked sourly at her. 'And when will that be?' she asked.

'It's difficult to say.' She glanced at the woman's face. It was impassive.

'I'm not rich,' said Mrs Smith. 'She'll have to be buried in Leek. I can't afford to have her body brought all the way down here. Expensive.'

It was neither the time nor the place but Joanna said it all the same. 'You will stand to inherit quite a bit of money from her estate as her next of kin, even if she died intestate.'

The woman looked at her scornfully. 'She was only a nurse,' she said. 'She won't have much – not if I know Marilyn. She always was a spender.'

Joanna was at a loss. It was Mike who chipped in.

'She did have a house, and a car.'

'Well, that's something,' she said, and they left it at that.

Suddenly Mrs Smith seemed to brighten. 'I'm forgetting my manners,' she said. 'You'd better come into the parlour.'

Joanna didn't think people still had parlours these days – chill, comfortless rooms with hard-backed chairs kept for best to impress. She followed Mrs Smith and Mike and sat down gingerly on the edge of an oak chair with a Rexine seat, while Mike stood near the door as though ready for escape.

She glanced around the room until her eyes rested on one of the few ornaments on the mantelpiece. It was a photograph of two newly qualified nurses on either side of a young man in a white coat. They looked a close trio, their arms entwined.

The plump girl with very dark hair was unmistakably Marilyn Smith. But the other?

Mrs Smith followed her glance. 'That's Pamella,' she said. 'She was Marilyn's best friend.' She jabbed her finger at the third figure in the white coat. 'She married him. He was a doctor. Marilyn works for him.' She stopped speaking. 'Worked for him,' she corrected. 'She *worked* for him. Of course that was taken a while ago.'

Joanna studied Pamella's face. Light brown hair, alive, sensitive, vivacious-looking. Very little make-up, perfect white teeth and pencil slim. It was easy to see why Jonah Wilson had fallen for her and not for the other young nurse in the photograph.

She decided it was time to ask some questions. 'I'm sorry,' she said, 'but we do need to ask just a few things.'

Mrs Smith looked immediately hostile. 'Whatever she got up to in her own time was her own affair. She was a big girl,' she added defensively, 'and always wilful.' Her dark eyes bored holes into Joanna. 'There wasn't much love lost between me and my daughter,' she said.

She perched uncomfortably on her chair, biting her lip. 'I don't really understand all this,' she said. 'Marilyn was never ill. How can she have died?' A hurt tone entered her voice. 'She was as strong as an ox. Why hasn't anybody explained? Will I have to travel all the way up there to the inquest?' She looked pained. 'All that expense . . .'

Joanna explained there was no real need for Mrs Smith to travel up to the inquest. At the same time she was unable to resist the comment that most parents would have wanted to travel to their daughter's inquest.

'But my arthritis . . .' Mrs Smith said, and Joanna, meeting Mike's amused eyes, gave up.

Bereavement had been the subject of one of Joanna's written examinations when she had had to discuss the telling of a family that one of their members had died suddenly. Then it had been purely theoretical – she had never done it. But now she knew – whatever emotion you described and laid at the feet of a recently bereaved person you could never be wrong.

She sighed and listened to Mrs Smith's whining voice, complaining about her daughter. 'Kept herself to herself . . . Never helped the family . . . After her father died she didn't care about me . . . Never visited. Never came to Cardiff.' Her tone became increasingly self-pitying.' I was always writing to her – a letter a week. She sent money, though – that was a help. But underneath she was a selfish little thing – always was.'

How many times had Joanna heard the disappointment parents feel when their children have not reached expectations? 'You wrote regularly?' she said.

Mrs Smith's angry eyes turned on her. 'You have to keep in touch,' she said. 'But she hardly ever wrote back. I didn't know how she was, what she was doing. I didn't have a clue. It was like I didn't have a daughter.'

Joanna glanced at Mike . . . It was like she didn't have a daughter. It was like the daughter didn't have a mother. Mike smiled.

Joanna was thinking of the letter she and Mike had read. Pages and pages of gossip, prying, intimate, insinuating gossip poured out on to paper. Mrs Smith had had nothing better to do with her time than peep through net curtains and observe the comings and goings of the neighbourhood. Like Evelyn, Mrs Smith's life had been seen through net curtains and windows. Vicariously. And her letters to Marilyn had been filled with it. Joanna felt a deep revulsion for this nosy woman who took such malicious delight in relaying the information to her daughter. And the daughter, Joanna thought. What had she really been like? A cruel manipulative nurse ... who had used her intimate knowledge of people to financial, greedy advantage?

Mrs Smith was glaring at her. 'So how did she die? Was it drink? Drugs? Where was she? Was she up to no good?'

Joanna cursed the uniformed locals. Had they told her so little? She forced herself to do her job. 'She died at home,' she said steadily, 'in bed and, it appears, alone.'

'She was too young for a heart attack,' the woman snapped.

Joanna met her eyes. 'The pathologist doesn't know what she died of.'

The woman's eyes grew round and incredulous. 'In this day and age? Well,' she said, 'he'd better find out. I'm her mother and I want to know how my daughter died.'

Joanna crossed the room and picked up the photograph of Marilyn Smith. No, even in this picture, in the flush of her success, she was not a pretty girl. There lurked something mean in the face that linked her to her mother.

'The coroner will hold the inquest as soon as the police, pathologist and forensic lab have ascertained all the facts,' she said.

Mrs Smith picked on one word. 'Forensic,' she repeated. 'Are you trying to say my daughter was murdered?'

'We don't know,' Joanna said patiently. 'We don't know how she died.'

A swift, calculating expression crossed Mrs Smith's face. 'When will her stuff be released, then?'

Joanna declined to comment. She was struggling to keep her temper. At the same time she was coming to the conclusion that Marilyn's mother was the most obnoxious woman she had ever met in her life.

'I can't say,' she said shortly. 'Soon – we hope. Mrs Smith . . . Do you think it is possible Marilyn might have committed suicide?'

'Hah.' Mrs Smith's expletive banished the thought. 'My daughter,' she said viciously, 'loved life. She wouldn't have wanted to die.' Her voice was defiant, challenging. 'She wouldn't have wanted to miss anything. I know my daughter did not commit suicide.' Something contemptuous entered her voice. 'She wouldn't have had the guts, Madame Policewoman.'

'Well, in that case it is possible – if we don't find a natural cause of death—' She stopped. It was against all police rules to mention this word before foul play could be proven. 'It could have been murder.'

'How?' Mrs Smith sounded angry.

'We don't know yet.' Joanna felt helpless. The frustration was eating at her. She knew the facts were lining up, underneath her fingertips. She simply wasn't able to read them.

Mrs Smith pressed her lips together and looked suddenly cunning and shrewd. 'You do think someone murdered Marilyn, don't you?'

'It's possible,' Joanna said. She gave Mrs Smith a contact telephone number, told her to ring if she remembered anything that might be significant and rose to leave. Mike followed her along the dingy hall. As she reached the front door she faced Mrs Smith again.

'We'll keep you informed,' she said. 'As soon as we know anything we'll be in touch.'

'Mind you do.' They were Mrs Vivian Smith's parting words.

All the way home in the car Joanna railed against Vivian Smith. 'What an absolute bitch,' she said. 'What a cow.'

'It isn't surprising, is it, that Marilyn turned out the way she did?'

Joanna was forced to agree.

It was after seven when Joanna finally unlocked the door of her cottage, slipped off her shoes and switched the answerphone on.

The first message was from Matthew. ' . . . Jo . . .' There was a long pause. She could hear him breathing. Then he said, 'Just rang to say hello,' and rang off.

The second was her mother. 'Joanna,' she said severely. 'We've heard absolutely nothing from you for almost two weeks. We don't know whether you're dead or alive.' Her voice softened. 'Come and see us when you've some spare time.' This Sunday, Joanna made a mental promise.

The third call was the duty sergeant. 'Evening, Inspector. Just thought you'd like to know Mrs Bloody Shiers has been on the blower all day long, complaining about the phantom dog.' There was a short pause and Joanna could hear someone whispering in the background. 'Willis says . . . have you heard the one about the phantom dog?' She groaned. ' . . . It did bark in the night.' Loud guffaws. 'See you in the morning, Inspector. Sweet dreams.'

The cat miaowed and leapt on to her lap. She felt too tired and depressed to push him off. Four days into the investigation and she was no closer to a solution than on day one. She still didn't know whether Marilyn had been murdered or not. She sighed. Maybe Mike was right. Perhaps because of her promotion she wanted this to be a murder case. Perhaps she was attaching too much importance to the anomalies in Marilyn's life. After all, there were skeletons in everybody's cupboards. Maybe she had had a married lover? – someone who was wealthy and willing to support her in the manner she so obviously loved.

She shivered a little and lit the fire, then sat down on the floor and started writing. Tomorrow . . . Willis to the bank. Get details of Marilyn's finances. Follow up the various acquaintances . . . Plenty to do.

So why did she feel depressed?

She sat for a few minutes, pondering, staring into the flames. What did she really want out of life . . .? Out of her job . . .? Out of relationships . . .?

Early on she had come to the conclusion that police work was incompatible with being a wife and mother. Hours too long and far too irregular. Besides, she didn't want children. She hated babies. She barely tolerated young dependants and could only really relate to rebellious teenagers – the more rebellious the better. And the job? She stared hard at the fire and knew she had contentment on that score. It was proving to be a good step in her life. The police force was for her.

Relationships . . .? That was the difficult one. There was only really Matthew. It wasn't simply his honey-coloured hair and his sharp green eyes. It was his intuitive intelligence . . . his wit. His presence of mind and the mental agility that seemed permanently switched on. She had been out with other cops during her career, but Matthew was simply – different. She and he had shared quick minds. She gave a wry smile. But Matthew had gone back to his wife and . . . She stood up. No doubt he shared a fulfilling relationship somewhere else. It was not with her. She gave a sigh. She'd better feed the cat.

'Come on, James,' she said, and he followed her into the kitchen, purring as he walked.

But as she opened the tin of cat food her mind could not leave the dead woman unexplained on the bed. She was uneasy with the case, and that was not the result of instinct but of training.

She poured boiling water on a teabag of Lapsang Souchong and carried it carefully back into the sitting room. Marilyn must have been expecting someone – a man. So who was it? The undertaker? She gave a soft giggle. What murky depths? For all the sinister nature of the man's work and a certain repugnance she felt for him physically, he did not seem a villain. And Marilyn had been possessed of a certain vicious intelligence. Joanna could not see the undertaker getting the better of her. Of the two,

114

Marilyn's mind had been the more devious. No, she decided then. The undertaker it was not. But she would still see him tomorrow.

The antique dealer? Give a dog a bad name, she thought. He was a bit too convenient – a ready-made villain and, she grudgingly conceded from Mike's account, clever, too. But the relationship between him and the dead nurse seemed, on the surface, remote. And would he have been able to pull off a murder that the pathologist could not recognize as such? She doubted it. He would have had no medical knowledge.

And Mrs Shiers. Why had she been so defensive about her husband? Was he dead? Was this terror of a phantom dog merely the manifestation of a guilty conscience? Joanna sat and pondered that one very carefully before deciding it was possible. Evelyn might conceivably have killed her husband and buried the body. On the surface she seemed an unlikely murderess. But murder can be no more than an accident. And she would be the sort of natural victim to panic after an accident . . . do something quite silly like bury the body in the garden. Perhaps he'd run off with someone else and wasn't really missing at all? She'd better speak to Mat in the morning – see if he had come up with anything. She grimaced.

Last of all she considered the unknown quantity: Dr Wilson. Of all the men involved Joanna did not want it to be him. She liked him.

'This is a puzzle,' she muttered, 'a dog rag puzzle.'

'Talking to yourself, Jo, is the first sign of madness.' The voice at the door made her jump.

'Tom . . . for goodness' sake!' She felt embarrassed, exposed.

'You a policewoman,' he said, 'and leaving the door open. Caro wanted me to come over and ask if you'd eat with us tonight.' Tom and Caro lived in the next cottage in the terrace. 'She's made a whacking great pot of curry – loads of rice.' He walked towards her. 'We'd both like you to come. We've been bickering all evening . . .'

'I haven't heard you,' she said.

'And you do usually . . .' He grinned. 'That's the trouble with these cottages. Walls do not have ears. They have microphones. Anyway – please come.'

'So Caro can pump me about the nurse?'

'Whatever the reason Caro wants you to come,' he said seriously, 'mine is purely for the joy of your company.'

Joanna smiled. 'How can I refuse?'

'Good.' Tom smiled back at her and reached for her hand with a quick, deft movement, then raised it to his lips. 'Thank you, Jo.' He made a face. 'I need some company with Caro tonight.'

'Why?' she asked.

He held his hand up, waved it around horizontally. 'Things none too good at the moment,' he said.

'Give me half an hour,' she said, 'and I'll bring the wine. And, Tom, don't worry about Caro. She does love you, you know.'

'No,' he said firmly, 'I do not know.'

She could hear Tom and Caro quarrelling as she knocked on the door, clutching a litre bottle of Chianti.

Tom's face was red, Caro's white. Both made a huge effort to pretend nothing was wrong and, as Joanna had thought, Caroline didn't waste much time before pumping her about the dead nurse.

Still, she enjoyed the evening. It was good to be in company again, to talk about things other than police work, when she could divert Caroline's mind away from the nurse's death.

'Had she had sex? Oh, come on, Jo,' she said at one point. 'You know I can find all this out by reading the coroner's report.'

'Then read it,' Joanna said. 'You know I can't tell you anything.'

'Yes, but what do you think?' she asked.

Joanna was tired. She'd drunk at least half a bottle of very nice Italian wine. She leaned forward. 'I'd lay a bet she was murdered,' she said.

Caro's eyes gleamed. 'I knew it.'

'You've done it now,' Tom muttered when Caro disappeared into the kitchen to pour the coffee. 'It'll be all over the local rag. Quote Detective Inspector Piercy is convinced Marilyn Smith was murdered unquote.' He looked at her kindly. 'You never learn about Caro, do you? For a copper, Joanna,' he said softly, 'you're bloody naive.'

They talked about the weather, and politics, and the latest show in Stoke's theatre in-the-round. The coffee sobered Joanna up and for the rest of the evening she was discretion itself.

But by that time the damage was done.

# Chapter 11

The story broke the following morning. 'Detective Inspector Piercy confided' – confided! Joanna would have liked to wring Caro's neck, and Tom's, too. The whole thing had been a set-up. She was furious as she read down the column.

'Detective Inspector Piercy confided in our reporter that her suspicions were that the dead nurse was murdered.'

Joanna finished the paragraph in disgust. Never again, she vowed. Never again do I make a friend of a newspaper person. She spent the next uncomfortable hour and a half on the carpet in the Chief Superintendent's office – 'I hope you can prove all this, Inspector' and references to how sad it was to begin her career on such a false note.

'And don't forget, Piercy, there were plenty who thought a woman might not be right for the job. We took a chance on you.' His beetling eyebrows lowered. 'Don't let me down, Piercy.' It was a threat.

Inwardly she groaned.

'Have you made any progress? It's four days since the woman died.'

'Not yet, sir.'

'You're an experienced police officer,' he said. 'We expect better than this from you. What makes you believe the poor woman was murdered, anyway?'

'Circumstances,' she said, and spent the next twenty minutes explaining the facts as she saw them. The blackmail . . . the clothes . . . the capsule.

He quickly saw the flaw in her argument. 'If she was waiting for a lover, why take a sleeping capsule?'

'I don't know, sir.'

He looked at her pityingly. 'In all probability, Piercy, she wasn't waiting for a lover at all.' He waved the wad of notes at her. 'And now we've got this bloody nutcase of a woman hearing phantom dogs.' He glared at her. 'She's ringing the station every five minutes complaining.'

'I'll go round and see her, sir,' she promised.

'And talking of dogs,' she said, 'if the bloody thing was as fierce as the report suggested surely nobody could have got past it.'

'I was going to talk to the vet later today, sir.'

'And, Piercy. Get Levin on the phone. Pin him down.'

'It's early days yet, sir.'

'Any other leads?'

'If you can spare Willis, sir, I thought I'd ask him to look into the bank accounts.'

His eyebrows almost met in the middle.

'I'm sure she was a blackmailer, sir.'

'All right,' he said. 'Keep Willis.'

He wagged his finger at her. 'One wrong-coloured capsule plus erotic underwear doesn't add up to murder.' He plucked at his chin. 'And by the way, Dr Wilson is very well thought of by the people of this town. Don't tread on his toes, or get in his way.' He cleared his throat noisily. 'He also happens to be my doctor. I don't want you upsetting him, please.'

She nodded.

'I'd like you to report to me after the weekend, Piercy. We'll review the situation then. And if the lab in Birmingham does uncover something and this turns out to be a simple overdose . . .'

'No, sir.'

He stared at her. 'You got carried away last night,' he said, almost kindly. 'In this job it can be very important knowing who you can trust and who you can't. Pick your friends carefully, Piercy. And in future. And for your sake,' he added, 'I just hope you're right. I don't think egg on your face would do much for your appearance.'

'No, sir.'

'By the way,' he said as she turned to go, 'how are you getting on with Korpanski?'

She looked at him suspiciously. 'We've had our differences,' she said cautiously, 'but I think we'll be all right.'

'Good,' he said. 'Good. Unfortunate about the paper,' he muttered, and she left.

En route to her own welcome office she passed Mike chatting to one of the DCs.

'Mike, can I have a word with you?'

He followed her into her office and stood in front of her desk, sharply to attention.

She sighed. 'No, not like that. I . . .' Words failed her. 'Sit down, Mike.'

He stood stiffly. 'I prefer to stand, thanks, Inspector.'

He looked tired this morning, irritable. The companionship they had enjoyed briefly yesterday seemed to have evaporated.

'I'd sort of hoped we could sit down over a coffee and discuss the case. The Superintendent is breathing down my neck. The article has upset him.'

'You might have phrased it better,' he said. 'You know the sort of thing . . . "Can't rule it out." I felt such a bloody fool reading that in the paper this morning.'

'I was at a private dinner party,' she said, 'with friends.'

'I'd change my friends, then,' he said grumpily. 'We'll look such a pair of idiots if it turns out she died naturally.'

'But she didn't,' Joanna insisted. 'You know she didn't.' She gazed at him. 'Something will crop up soon. We still don't know who she was expecting that night. Nor do we know where her money came from. I just want to find out the truth. I really do have a feeling, Mike.'

He grunted. 'The Super doesn't have a lot of faith in feelings. He deals in hard facts, Inspector, as do we all. We're the police, Joanna, not mediums, and I'd lay a bet she wasn't expecting anyone.'

She felt her irritation grow. 'I know that's what you think, Mike,' she said, 'but one hard fact we do not have is the cause of death. Without that . . .' She looked at him sharply. 'Are you all right?'

He looked sheepish. 'Wife giving me a hard time,' he muttered.

'Oh.' She felt inadequate. 'I'm sorry. Is it the hours?'

'Not really,' he said. 'She's just being bloody stupid.' He shifted uncomfortably. 'There was a picture,' he said. 'Fran saw it.' He grinned. 'You look a bit less like a gypsy than usual. It's a good photo and my wife can be a bit jealous.'

'I'm sorry,' she said. 'I don't know where the picture came from.' Then she remembered. Caro and Tom playing with a new camera, a few months ago at a barbecue. And she was suddenly bitterly resentful. She had counted them among her small circle of friends. If they could not be trusted, then who? Problems from the men in the force she had anticipated. But this . . .?

'It's not as if you're married,' he carried on. 'It wouldn't be so bad then. If you had a husband. But single . . .'

Now she was furious. 'I'm not bloody well getting married so your wife can sleep well at nights, Mike,' she said. 'If she feels I'm a threat well I'm bloody sorry. You're just going to have to convince her, Mike. It's her problem.'

'It's mine too.'

She looked at him. He looked fed up and tired. She gave a lopsided grin. 'Having a hard time, Korpanski? Wife giving you a hard time?'

'Bugger off,' he said, laughing.

'Come on,' she said. 'We've got work to do. It's hard enough without these extra problems.'

'You know,' he said, 'if this was a detective novel Agatha Christie would have used a vegetable alkaloid.'

'I've thought of that,' she admitted. 'Perhaps I had better speak to Matthew Levin again. The trouble is, Mike,' she said, 'we all know that without the cause of death we know nothing. That has to be our starting point.'

She stabbed the point of her pen into the paper. 'The cause of death.'

She looked at Mike. 'Perhaps the Super's right. We're really getting nowhere.' She picked up her coffee and stared into the bottom of the cup.

Mike bent over her. She could feel his breath on the back of her neck. 'You'll just have to lean on your pet pathologist, madam.'

Joanna spoke awkwardly. 'I don't feel it's the right approach at the moment. I feel we should pursue other enquiries.'

Mike moved away. 'If you say so, Inspector.' He looked at her carefully. 'Joanna,' he said tentatively, 'don't let your personal prejudices interfere.'

She looked questioningly at him.

'If it wasn't Dr Levin,' he said, 'you'd have been on the blower by now, badgering him for a cause of death. You'd have made a right nuisance of yourself. You wouldn't have side-stepped the issue.'

'I know you're right, Mike. And I will ring him.'

'So what else is on the agenda?'

She ticked off her list. 'I want Willis to go to the bank to get some details. It's time we looked into Marilyn's financial affairs a bit closer. Over the last two years, I think.'

'And you?'

'I've got plenty to do, Mike,' she said. 'I think it's about time I called on our Mr Machin. Check him out. I'd like to meet him anyway. And then there's Dr Wilson. He hasn't exactly told us the truth, the whole truth and nothing but the truth, has he? What's your gut feeling?'

He frowned. 'I don't know. I get the impression here the answer could be just about anything. I honestly don't know.'

She grinned and held out her hand. 'Like to take a bet?'

'I know what you'd put a tenner on.'

She nodded. 'You're right.'

'OK,' he said. 'You stick to your murder theory. Ten quid says it's suicide.' They shook hands.

Joanna sighed. 'I suppose I really ought to visit our friend Evelyn too.' She made a face. 'I can't wait to meet this phantom dog.'

'I'll come with you, Joanna,' he said. 'I'd like to meet her.' He watched her curiously. 'Do you think she could have killed her husband?'

Joanna shrugged her shoulders. 'At first I would have said no. Now, I'm not quite so sure.'

She was still thinking when she backed the car out of the space. Her first murder case as an inspector. Why couldn't it have been straightforward? Why did it have to be such a tricky business? And now she had to move forward in this case or drop it. By Monday, the Super had said, then she had to return to the drugs through schools problem. 'The county can't afford to watch you running around in circles, making a fool of yourself, finding out nothing, quoted in newspapers and listening to hunches,' the Super had said. 'Set an example. Teach the young rookies when to hold on to a case and when to let go. It's obvious this girl died from natural causes and the doctors just haven't been quite thorough enough.'

She had demurred. What about the clothing?

'She was just a kinky cow, Detective Inspector. No more than that. You'll find it's nothing more than drugs and alcohol. Until Monday – and that's it.'

But there were people she wanted to speak to first. She had a sudden thought. So far all the connections had been men . . . Marilyn had been fond of men.

She turned to Mike. 'All men,' she said. 'Machin, Paul Haddon, Dr Wilson. No women friends. Surely everyone has women friends. Where were Marilyn's?'

'The doctor's wife?'

She nodded. 'That's what I think. They were close, weren't they?'

'What about Mrs Shiers?'

They stood outside the neat bungalow. Nets twitched. She was watching for them.

She must have recognized Joanna because the door opened as soon as she mounted the front step.

Evelyn Shiers – even more like a cornered, bristling fox than ever – stared suspiciously at Mike. 'Who's he?' she asked.

'Detective Sergeant Korpanski, Mrs Shiers.' Joanna glanced at Mike. 'We understand that you're still being disturbed by a dog barking.'

Evelyn glared at her. 'It wasn't just any dog, Inspector. I told you. It was Ben. I heard him. I know his bark.'

Joanna shot another swift glance at Mike. 'We need to look round your garden,' she said.

The woman looked nervous. 'What for . . . Why?'

'To look for the dog,' Mike said stolidly. 'You see we believe you, Mrs Shiers.'

Reluctantly Evelyn led the way round the back to the garden. There was no doubt – the garden was overlooked by Marilyn's house, was dominated by it. Three side windows gave on to Evelyn's small patch. Although it was spring little was coming to life here. The cats had overrun the garden as they had the house. Joanna walked the length of the patch. Jock Shiers had disappeared four years ago. At the end of the garden was a small, flowering tree. Joanna stopped in front of it. It was young – could not have been growing more than a few years. Nailed to its base was a crude wooden cross. She looked enquiringly at Evelyn.

The woman was pale with terror. Her eyes were filling with tears. Her hand shook as she crossed herself.

'Cat,' she said hoarsely. 'My cat. He died.'

The two police looked at each other. Joanna glanced at the base of the tree and muttered to Mike, 'Do we dig?'

Imperceptibly he nodded then turned to Evelyn. 'I don't hear a dog,' he said.

Evelyn held her hands up to her ears. 'The dog,' she said. 'I can hear it.' She looked from one to the other. 'Can't you?'

'Look,' Joanna said kindly. 'I think . . . I think all this

has been a strain on you. Why don't you see a doctor?'

And to Mike later, when they were back in the car, she said, 'What if she was blackmailing her too?'

He objected. 'But Jock Shiers disappeared before Marilyn lived here.'

Joanna stared through the windscreen. 'I don't know, Mike. What if she sort of ... tended the grave and Marilyn saw her?'

He nodded. 'Possible.'

'And ... blackmailed her. It would explain the phantom dog. Disturbed, guilty mind "hears" the dog ... Remember Ben was put down because Marilyn died.'

'Just one or two tiny flaws in your case, Joanna,' he said. 'One, if you're suggesting Evelyn Shiers actually killed Marilyn, she was bloody terrified of that dog. She'd never have got past him. And two, we still don't know how Marilyn died.'

Joanna was silent for a moment then murmured, 'Poisoned meat?' She sighed. 'We need to talk to the vet. Right now, Mike, I think I'll go and visit your friend Grenville Machin.'

'Yes – let's,' he said, but she put a hand on his arm.

'I think I'd rather go on my own. I don't want to antagonize him and I think you're probably a bit of a red rag to that particular bull, Mike.'

'You spoil all the fun,' he grumbled.

'I know ... I know. Look – why don't you go and see the vet again? Ask him whether he thinks Ben might have allowed anyone into the house.'

Mike gave a grin. 'You want me to ask about phantom dogs while I'm there?'

She laughed. 'Why not?'

The antique shop was huge – a massive warehouse converted into a showroom of antiques all shapes and sizes. Joanna walked in and was met by a tiny, strikingly pretty blonde behind the counter. She wore a skintight, black Lycra miniskirt with high-heeled silver boots and a scarlet silk shirt which showed small, pointed breasts. She raised thick, black false eyelashes at Joanna. 'Can I help you?'

Joanna showed her her ID card. 'I'm Detective Inspector Piercy,' she said. 'I'm investigating the death of Marilyn Smith.' She looked at the blonde, who had shrewd, business eyes in spite of the bimbo costume. 'Did you know her?'

The girl bit her lip. 'I don't think so,' she said slowly.

Joanna drew out the photograph she had of the dead nurse. 'Have a look at this...'

'Patty,' the girl supplied. 'Patty Brownlow.' She stared at the picture then raised the heavy lashes. 'I don't think so,' she said, then scrutinized Joanna's face. 'What did you say your name was?'

Joanna gave it again and the blonde disappeared to find Grenville Machin, leaving Joanna with the vague feeling she might meet Patty Brownlow again.

He was nothing like she had expected. No hint of the thug millionaire. He was short – a few inches shorter than she – slim, almost weedy, with a heavy Italianate moustache, bristly like a lavatory brush. He held out his hand and gave her a charming, suave smile, displaying white, wolfish teeth.

'What can I do for you, Detective Inspector? A woman...' He leered '...and so far in her chosen profession.' His eyes crinkled. 'No stopping you now, is there?'

And all the time she was wondering, is this man a clever murderer? Joanna felt a deep revulsion for him with his easy confidence. Dislike doesn't necessarily make a man a criminal, but she knew this one was, one way or another... Drugs... Stolen goods... Fraud... Attempted murder? Murder?

She took a deep breath. 'I'm investigating the sudden death of Marilyn Smith.' She used the word 'sudden' purposely, hoping to rattle him. It failed. He merely looked puzzled.

'Who?' he asked.

'Sister Marilyn Smith,' Joanna said clearly. 'She worked at the Health Centre. She was found dead on Tuesday, at home. I believe you were a close friend of hers.'

Grenville Machin looked completely comfortable. 'Then you've been misinformed,' he said. 'I'm afraid, Inspector, that someone has been telling you little porkies.'

'Porkies?'

'Pork pies,' he said. 'Lies.'

Round one to him, she thought.

'But you did know her?'

He sauntered to the window, doodled in the dust on the windowpane, then turned so his face was in deep shadow, features in darkness. 'No better than I know a few hundred of my other regular customers,' he said. 'I sold her some nice pieces of furniture over the years. I even delivered them to her house.' He smiled carelessly. 'I do that for most of my private customers. Of course – trade . . .' He shrugged his shoulders and bared his teeth again, stroking his moustache lovingly. 'When probate has been settled I'd be quite happy to buy most of them back. They were honest pieces,' he said, his black eyes flashing with a rude challenge.

Now Joanna knew why Mike had such a strong abhorrence for the man. He was an utter rat. As a woman she felt her skin prickle in reaction to him; any red-blooded man would long to punch him.

'We need to examine the circumstances surrounding her death,' she said sharply, 'before we sell off her household goods.'

The antique dealer grinned. 'No harm in trying,' he said. 'It'll have to go somewhere and I'm offering.'

'I suggest you were close friends.' She kept her eyes trained on his face, which was screwed up against the light, trying to draw what she could from his dark features.

But Grenville Machin laughed at her. 'Close friends!' he exploded. 'Do you mean what I think you mean?

God,' he said, 'you've seen her. She was no oil painting. Now Patty there...' He jerked his head towards the blonde, just visible through the open door. 'That's what I call pretty – worth a grunt or two.' His face challenged her and she felt a sudden, hot anger.

'I've seen Marilyn Smith dead,' she said. 'No one is pretty dead.' But she knew it had the ring of truth. The blonde and Marilyn Smith were women out of two quite different moulds. Try as hard as she might, she knew Grenville had not been the man Marilyn Smith had bought black lace for. But there had been no actual love-making. What if it had all been in Marilyn's mind? What if Grenville Machin had led her on, pretended he found her attractive? What if he had decided on a way to deal with the blackmailer?

But she knew what rankled. This man was trying to make her look a fool and was succeeding in nettling her. The connection between the dead woman and this buyer and seller of fine antiques was tenuous. Possibly they hardly knew each other. More make believe?

But... 'How did she pay for her pieces?' she asked.

Grenville Machin looked momentarily discomfited. 'I can't remember,' he said irritably. 'It was a couple of years ago.' He leered and his confidence seeped back. 'I sell a load of stuff through this place,' he said. 'I can't be expected to remember how everybody pays for them.'

'But you keep books,' Joanna insisted.

'I have to,' he said. 'Inland Revenue.'

'I'd be grateful, Mr Machin,' she said calmly, 'if you'd hunt out the receipts of the antiques you sold to Marilyn Smith. We know about the clock and the bureau.' She smiled smoothly. 'Was there anything else?'

He was rattled. He reddened and promised to have the books ready for inspection by the following day. Joanna stood up to leave but underneath her confident manner she was depressed. She felt disheartened and tired and sickened by Machin.

'I've read about you,' he needled. 'Got a bee in your

bonnet about murder. I don't suppose it's occurred to you that maybe she died in her sleep. You coppers,' he said, 'see murderers hiding round every tree, behind every door. We're all crooks to you, ain't we?'

She tightened her lips and he grinned even more broadly. 'Keep your hair on,' he said. 'Pretty woman like you. You should be married – at home with a couple of kids, not pitting your wits against the criminal world.'

'Mr Machin,' she said sharply, 'you sound just like my mother.' She put her tongue in her cheek. 'Would you mind if I had a quick look round? I believe you export Doulton figures to the United States.' She looked hard at him. 'We have a lot of thefts in the Potteries of Doulton figures. I don't suppose there's any connection.'

He looked wary. 'Got a warrant?'

'No,' she said smoothly, 'but I have a penchant for antiques. I just might want to buy some.'

The antique dealer looked furious and she knew she had emerged the victor of this minor skirmish.

'Don't go through any of the doors marked private,' he snarled. 'I've got closed-circuit television.'

She tutted. 'The things we have to do these days to deal with the criminal fraternity.'

After about an hour she had seen enough. He saw her to the door.

'Call again,' he said.

'Unfortunately I'm not terribly fond of cheap Far Eastern imports,' she said. 'But I do like antiques.' She glanced around. 'I don't seem to have spotted many.'

He scowled. 'They aren't so easy to get hold of these days,' he muttered and she stared at him.

'But you let Marilyn Smith have some.'

He kicked the step. 'She paid me a good price.'

'Prove it,' she said. 'I'm not sure I believe you. By the way, Mr Machin . . .' she added, 'fond of dogs, are you?'

He stared at her. 'Now what are you on about?'

'Just asking,' Joanna said coolly.

He frowned. 'One thing I've learned in my dealings

with your lot,' he said. 'You never "just ask" anything.'

'Exactly.'

On the way back to the station she decided it was time to call again at the doctor's surgery and was met this time by an empty waiting room and the red-haired receptionist about to pull the shutter down. She didn't look in the least bit pleased to see Joanna. 'He's just finished,' she said. 'He's had a long day. I hope you haven't got a lot of questions.'

'Just one or two.'

The receptionist spoke on the telephone then turned back to her. 'He'll be with you in a moment.'

Joanna picked up a magazine and leafed through it, feeling the familiar nervous prickling associated with the smell of disinfectant and methylated spirits. It had been a long time since she had sat, nervously waiting, in a doctor's surgery, for the results of a test, worry gnawing away her stomach. She needn't have worried – it had been negative and that had been the last time she had visited her own doctor. 'Worry,' the doctor had said, 'can cause the same symptom.' She had not known whether to laugh or cry and in the end she had got drunk – alone. That had been two years ago.

'Damn this whole bloody case,' she muttered. Why didn't crime ever take her to a glamorous hotel for some show-biz, film-star luxury? Instead she was here, staring at walls that warned of HIV and advised her to check her tetanus status, reading two-year-old magazines.

She looked up and saw the doctor. He didn't look pleased to see her either and he gave her a quick, embarrassed glance. She joined him in the reception area just as he was shutting the door of the safe.

'Prescription pads,' he explained, 'plus some of the more sensitive sets of notes.'

She wondered whose were the 'sensitive' notes.

Jonah would be cross. She had opened the garage and

found a large screwdriver with a yellow plastic handle. Then she had climbed the stairs, hearing Stevie's naughty giggling getting louder with each step. She had pushed the screwdriver hard in and the door had splintered and cracked. Then she was afraid – afraid to go in and afraid of what she might find. So she sat on the top step, holding the screwdriver tightly in her fist.

'Stevie . . .' she whispered, ' . . . Stevie.'

He turned to Joanna and gave her a tired smile. With a shock she realized he looked ten years older. Was it the death of his nurse? The extra work? The strain? She hardly thought so. It was something else.

'What can I do for you, Inspector?'

'I wanted to go over Marilyn's last day here,' she said. 'Was she excited about something that day, happy, pleased – different in any way?'

The doctor thought, blinked and frowned. 'No, I don't think so,' he said. 'She seemed the same as ever.'

Joanna turned to Sally. 'Did you notice anything on that particular day? Did anything unusual happen? A telephone call? A letter?'

The receptionist looked away. 'Not really,' she said, busying herself filing notes.

The doctor looked at her. 'Why?' he asked. 'What's turned up?'

But Joanna found herself reluctant to discuss the case with either of them. There was something conspiratorial – guilty even – between the pair. She looked from one to the other.

'Nothing. I wanted really to tell you we still haven't found the cause of death. It's possible we might drop the case. 'Did she imagine that look of relief, or was she seeing spectres where there were none?

'Of course,' she added, 'we might find something out from the forensic lab in Birmingham.'

It was not her imagination. The wary look was back again.

131

The doctor looked strained. 'She has to have died from natural causes,' he said. 'Why involve the Birmingham lab?'

'We requested some of the internal organs be sent there for analysis,' she said formally, and wondered why he looked so upset. The next minute she felt sorry for him. He looked pale and so tired – ready to drop – and he had known the dead woman for a number of years; they had been colleagues – and once friends.

'Did any of you ever see Marilyn swallow any capsules?' she asked, 'red and yellow ones. Did she ever mention any medication she was prescribed?'

'I should ask Dr Bose,' he said.

'We have.' Joanna paused. 'He wasn't prescribing her anything. Tell me, Doctor, did Marilyn have access to drugs here in the surgery?'

'Of course.' He sounded impatient. 'Inspector, she was my nurse. She had access to absolutely anything she wanted.' He ran his fingers through his hair. 'I had to trust her.' He frowned. 'Red and yellow capsules sound like an antibiotic,' he said. 'Hold on. I'll look it up.'

A minute or so later, he said, 'There's a penicillin preparation in a red and yellow capsule.'

'Was she taking penicillin?' Joanna asked innocently.

Doctor and receptionist shook their heads. 'Not that we know of. I never saw her take pills.'

Joanna stood up to leave. 'We'll keep you informed.' She hesitated. 'Dr Wilson, would you mind if I spoke to your wife?'

He wheeled round. 'What on earth has all this business got to do with Pam? I told you. My wife isn't well. She's a vulnerable woman. News like this will upset her.'

'You mean she doesn't know about Marilyn's death?' said Joanna in disbelief. 'You haven't told her?'

Jonah Wilson shook his head. 'Why should she know?' he asked. 'It doesn't affect her.'

She was taken aback by his manner and by the receptionist's vigorous nodding. They were protecting Pamella Wilson as though she were a child. Why shield her from the news? Would it upset her so very much?

'But they were friends,' she said. 'Good friends. Best friends.'

The doctor looked at her curiously, and said quickly, 'She can't help you. They trained together in the same hospital. They were friends then but since Pamella and I were married . . .'

'But they were still friends after you were married.' She paused. 'Do you mean it was after your wife's illness?'

The doctor nodded. 'She knows nothing. I promise you, Inspector.' He was pleading. 'My wife is a sick woman – very sick. I don't want her upset.'

'Dr Wilson,' Joanna said gently. 'I don't want your wife upset either. But I must speak to her. I honestly believe she might be able to help.'

'The damned tart . . .' Jonah Wilson finally lost his self-control. 'Pamella . . .' He covered his face with his hands. 'She doesn't know a thing about it.'

'About what?'

'About anything.'

'I'm sorry,' she said, 'but I must insist. I only need to confirm the times you were out on Monday night and ask her a few questions about Marilyn.'

'She hadn't even seen her for years.'

'They might have talked on the phone.'

'Pamella would have told me,' he said. 'She hides nothing from me.'

'I'll deal with her sensitively,' Joanna said, but the doctor gave a dry laugh.

'Sensitively,' he echoed. 'The police?'

Joanna swallowed her pride and her anger. It was a large mouthful . . .

Jonah suddenly met her eyes. 'It was years ago that she knew Marilyn. They hadn't seen each other for a long time. She won't miss Marilyn, you know. If you need to know about my night visits you can ask the receptionists here.' He was panicking. 'All night visits are filled in on the notes – times as well.'

'Just a minute,' she said. 'Do you mean you come here,

pick up the notes and then visit the patient?'

He shook his head. 'We fill in the night visit pad then stick it in the notes.'

Joanna nodded. 'I see,' she said. 'Times as well?'

'We have to,' he said reluctantly. 'It makes a difference how much we're paid – night visit rate.'

She fixed her gaze on the doctor. 'You should have told me your wife and Marilyn were friends,' she said.

'I wanted to keep her out of it.'

'But it was through your wife that Marilyn came to work here.'

He nodded. 'Look,' he said. 'If you must see Pam I'd rather it was when I'm with her.'

'When?'

He picked up his coat. 'I'm on my way home,' he said diffidently. 'Does now suit?'


The house was the first surprise, a modest 1930s semi with a tiny garden and peeling paintwork. Pamella Wilson was the second.

Even as Jonah turned his key in the door he called out to her to warn her he was not alone. 'I'm home, darling, and somebody's with me. Don't be alarmed ... Pam, it's a policewoman ... Don't worry ...'

Mrs Wilson emerged from behind the living room door, peeping round like a shy child, small and thin with huge dark eyes and a screwed-up face, as though she was about to ask a question. She looked vulnerable, frightened. She was so pathetic a figure, Joanna felt nothing but pity.

Pamella Wilson held out a large yellow screwdriver. 'I'm sorry,' she said to Jonah. 'I'm so sorry.'

He took the screwdriver from her very gently. 'Oh, Pam,' he said. 'Don't go in there any more.'

Two large tears rolled down her face. 'I just wanted to see him, Jonah,' she said. 'I thought he would be there.'

He turned helplessly to Joanna. 'Let me talk to her alone for five minutes,' he said. 'Let me tell her about Marilyn in my own way, please – explain ...'

Joanna was moved. It was almost as though his wife was a patient and he was telling her she had a few months left to live. She waited in the hall. The heavy-booted approach would never work here. Here was a woman who would crumble faced with interrogation. But she had also been the only woman Joanna had met who had even claimed to be a friend of the dead nurse.

Jonah opened the door and peered out. 'I don't have to ask you – be sensitive, Inspector. My wife is not well.'

Pamella was sitting hunched in an upright chair, facing the window and rocking slightly.

'Mrs Wilson,' she said softly and pulled up a twin chair to face her.

'Died in her sleep,' Pamella murmured, looking at Joanna. 'Jonah told me Marilyn died in her sleep.' She looked towards Joanna with weary eyes. 'Sometimes I wish I could die in my sleep too. My baby died in its sleep,' she said. 'Did you know?' She stopped suddenly. 'He was a beautiful baby. Everybody loved him. Everybody loved my Stevie.'

Joanna did not know what to say. She could not remember feeling so inadequate. God, was her first panicking thought. I can get no help from this woman. She cannot know anything. I've made another mess. Annoyed this poor, busy doctor – and his ruined wife.

Pamella spoke again. 'Marilyn and I were friends,' she said. 'Did you know we were friends?'

'Yes,' Joanna said cautiously. 'That's why I'm here.' She watched Pamella very carefully. 'When did you last see Marilyn, Mrs Wilson?'

A shaft of cunning struck the woman's face. 'I don't think I can remember . . .' She paused. 'No – I'm quite sure I can't remember.' She tugged at Joanna's sleeve.

Somewhere nearby a vodaphone rang. Jonah pulled it out of his pocket. 'On call,' he explained. 'I'll take it in the kitchen.' He looked anxiously at his wife. 'Will you be all right?'

She nodded and Jonah left, his wife following him with

her dark, sad eyes. 'We didn't like her,' she said. 'She wasn't very nice.' It took Joanna a second or two to realize it was Marilyn she was referring to.

'Really?' she asked. 'In what way?'

Pamella Wilson leaned forwards. 'He should have given her the sack, got rid of her when she first started,' she whispered. 'We thought she would be a help to us.' She shook her head. 'But she wasn't. She damned us. She was trouble—'

Joanna interrupted. 'In what way was she trouble, Mrs Wilson?'

Pamella began to rock again in the chair, rhythmically to and fro. 'She mocked us,' she said. 'Mocked us.' And then that cunning look was back. 'She wanted to take my Jonah away from me, you know.'

Joanna did not know what to say.

Pamella nodded. 'She did,' she said. 'She wanted my Jonah. What she didn't know was that she couldn't have him. Jonah would never have left me. Never. Do you understand, Mrs Pretty Policewoman?'

Joanna did understand – only too well. You could not take a man from his wife. Yes . . . she knew.

'Jonah always was soft and very kind to her,' Pamella continued. 'And it made her think she had a chance.' She smiled and hugged her knees. 'But she didn't.' There was a look of complete triumph on the woman's face.

Joanna stared. It was an ugly look.

Pamella's skirt was brown, loose and very saggy, her sweater bottle green, covered in splinters of wood. She wore no make-up, was pale and lined and she looked ill. Her feet, in loose dark slippers, were knotted around the legs of the chair. How could the doctor work with sick patients all day and come home to this?

Jonah Wilson wandered back into the room and kissed his wife.

'I have to go now,' he said, then looked directly at Joanna. 'You have finished, haven't you?'

It was a dismissal.

# Chapter 12

'I want to get him, Mike,' she said.

He looked at her. 'Who?'

'Machin.'

'You don't think . . .?'

She leaned forward, chin cupped in her hand, and stared straight into Mike's face. 'I don't know,' she said. 'The trouble is I can't see how he could have done it.' She laughed. 'Call it a copper's instinct, Mike,' she said. 'He's a crook. I want to see him put away.'

'How?' He stood up, agitated, pacing the room. 'Look, Joanna,' he said. 'We've been trying for ages. He's been getting steadily richer and richer over the last six, seven years. We've never managed to pin a thing on him, at least nothing that would stand up in court.' He stared at her, frowning. 'You know how frustrating it can be . . . all that police work – for nothing. And you know the defence will make a total fool of you, make you out to be corrupt, victimizing an innocent man. And that's if it gets past the Crown Prosecution Service. Joanna, we have to catch him with blood on his hands.'

'Not blood,' she said. 'Not blood.'

'What, then?'

'Come on, Mike,' she said impatiently. 'We know where all that money came from. And it's bloody obvious – the connection with Marilyn Smith.'

'I'm sorry,' he said politely. 'I don't think we're talking the same language any more.'

'Drugs!' she said. 'Containers full of antiques. And

what else? Drugs. What better vehicle to smuggle drugs into the country? We should have thought of him before. Why has he kept so quiet for the last couple of years? Besides – who better than a dealer to be handling all those stolen china figures? I want a check made on the Doulton found in Marilyn's house. We can make a start on handling stolen goods. Then we'll take it from there.'

'You'll never prove it,' he said. 'And even if you could you couldn't make it stick.'

'We'll make it stick,' she said grimly. 'That and a murder charge.'

Mike bit his lip and watched her.

She turned back to her notes. 'I don't suppose Jock Shiers has turned up?'

'No such luck. And no record of the *Marie Celeste* in Bangor. No one's seen either the boat or him. The coastguard doesn't know it.'

'Do you mean the boat is missing or that it was never there?'

'It was registered,' he said, 'but not from North Wales. South Wales – Milford Haven.'

'And,' she said.

'And nothing... No one seems to know anything about it.'

She sat very still. 'He's disappeared, Mike...' She looked up at him. 'He's disappeared, hasn't he?'

'So far,' he said uneasily.

'Do we have a description?'

'Heavily built,' he muttered, 'aged fifty, no scars. Black hair.'

She sighed. 'Not a lot of help.'

She stood up. 'I'm getting a warrant,' she said, suddenly decisive. She badly needed the action. 'We're digging up the bloody garden. You saw her, Mike,' she said defensively. 'Something's under that cross.'

'Look,' he said. 'We have a prime suspect. Why go preying on her?'

'There's something there,' she said.

He moved towards her, even more uneasy now.

'Joanna,' he said awkwardly. 'Don't think I'm trying to tell you your job.'

The hardness was back in her eyes. She knew what he was going to say.

'Don't you think you should have a word with Dr Levin?' He paused. 'If only we could get some idea of what she died of . . .'

'I want to leave him out of this,' she said, 'as much as possible.'

'But—'

She wheeled around. 'I'm not ringing Matthew,' she said. 'And that's that.'

Mike scowled and she felt angry with him – and with herself. But she did not want to ring him. She wanted him to ring her.

The telephone rang as if on cue, and she stared at it.

It was Evelyn Shiers, and this time she was hysterical. 'Come and listen!' she said. 'Listen to him. Then you'll know . . . He sniffs around the tree.'

Joanna let the woman rant for a full five minutes then she put the phone down and sat for a while, still holding the receiver, before she made her decision.

'I want the garden dug up,' she said, 'concentrating on the bit around the willow tree.'

Mike said nothing. He watched her carefully. She knew he wanted to speak. Just as surely as she knew he would probably say nothing unless she prompted him.

'All right,' she said eventually, 'go on. What's bugging you?'

He leaned back in the chair. 'I don't see Evelyn Shiers killing anyone,' he said. 'Least of all her husband. And if she had killed him, she wouldn't have carried on living there. She couldn't have.'

'What else would she have done?' Joanna demanded. 'Confess? Sell the house and have someone digging up the garden? What else?'

'She couldn't have lived there with him lying in the garden for years.'

Joanna's hand touched the telephone. 'Stranger things

have happened,' she said. 'Besides, why the hysterics?'

He shook his head. 'Panic?'

'I don't think so.' She picked up the telephone. 'We'll soon see,' she said, waiting for the connection. She spoke quickly into it, justifying her reasons for the request.

When she had finished Mike stood up. 'And Machin?'

'He'll have to wait.' She paused, hoping she might gain his approval. When he remained silent she spoke again.

'It is a murder investigation,' she said. 'We'll get back to him.'

He stood over her so his eyes were very close to hers. 'And Dr Levin?'

She broke the gaze, picked up her coat. 'He can wait too.'

It was dull and grey, no sign of sun, just interminable drizzle.

Joanna picked up one of the spades and started to dig. The soil stuck to the spade so she had to shake off each clod. Her hands were cold and muddy. She looked around at the silent, digging group. Police work, she thought. Neither glamorous nor romantic.

She looked up to see Evelyn watching through the window, a dark shape, shadowy and silent. Joanna stared at her and knew she would never forget the woman's expression when she had knocked on the door and told her they would dig up the garden. She had looked as though she had given up all hope, a lost, unhappy woman who had lived for years with a guilty, lonely secret, one which her next door neighbour had capitalized on. She had blinked with her frightened pale eyes and muttered something about a migraine. And now she stood, motionless at the window, staring down at the diggers.

Grave diggers, Joanna thought, and dug again into the stiff clay. She looked up to see Evelyn standing at her side, clutching a coat around her.

'Why?' she asked.

'Because we're curious about the whereabouts of your

140

husband,' Joanna said. 'There isn't anything you'd like to add, is there, before we carry on?'

Evelyn's face hardened. She looked at Joanna with dislike. 'It isn't your business,' she said. 'What happened to my husband is nothing to do with you.' She looked around the square, muddy lawn. 'He isn't here, you know.'

Then the quick, brave moment passed and the frightened fox was back. 'Find the dog,' she said. 'Find out where Ben's barking from.'

'While we dig,' Joanna said stolidly. 'While we dig we'll listen.'

Evelyn stomped back into the house.

She was left with eight sturdy volunteers. The Super had proved generous. Men had appeared from other divisions. Murder was a serious crime. No manpower problems in this case.

'Get this solved,' he had said. 'Dig up the secrets, Piercy, and find out how and why this wretched woman died.'

The press had been short of news recently. The original story had been followed up on page two by indignant headlines. 'Police no further ... Detective Inspector Piercy unavailable for comment ...' Joanna had grimaced as she had read it. 'Unavailable for comment ...' 'But it is understood they still cannot rule out homicide.'

Dig ... dig ... dig ... The sound of the scrabbling of the shovel against clods of earth liberally peppered with gravel and stones. They squared the garden with red plastic tape to show where they had already investigated. If they did find Jock Shiers' body it would be allocated one of the squares ... D4 ... C3 ... Joanna sighed. They had begun near the willow tree and fanned out. The drizzle was filling small channels with mud. Her wellington boots were sucked into the squelch. She needed a bath.

Her spade touched something hard. She peered down. Not caring any more about the mud on her hands, her knees ... she fumbled in the ground and pulled out a bone.

It was strange to watch the diggers. They had been mechanical, careful but bored by the job. Now their spades quickened. As Mike used the car phone to ring the pathologist they worked to uncover the bones. Joanna glanced across at the house. The face had gone. Evelyn was no longer watching.

It took Matthew almost an hour to arrive at the scene, by which time they had cleared the earth around a small collection of bones. Joanna's face was smeared with mud. And she was cold. The light was fading and she was achingly tired. She heard Matthew's car pull up the drive, then the crunch of his feet up the garden path, the squeak of the gate. She looked up.

He gave her a quick, amused glance which told her she looked a mess. She wiped her face and smeared more mud across her cheek.

'What have you got?' he said, and she pointed to the pile of bones.

He squatted down, picked up first one long bone then another and as he touched the skull she felt suddenly foolish. He studied it for a minute then grinned at her. 'Dog,' he said, setting it down next to the others. 'Did you find any more?'

She knew then the effort in the garden had been wasted. She watched the diggers. They had covered nearly the whole garden. Wherever Jock Shiers was he was not lying here. She straightened up. Matthew's hand was on her shoulder. She knew from his touch he felt her humiliation. And she knew he was excited about something. 'I've been trying to get in touch with you all day,' he said. 'I've got some news.'

'At last,' she said, 'some light.'

Matthew grinned. 'Don't get too excited, Jo,' he warned. 'I haven't proved it yet but I'm optimistic.'

She felt a surge of warmth for him. 'I could hug you,' she said.

142

He stared at her then and she caught her breath at the fierce, hot expression in his face.

He drew a handkerchief out of his pocket, wiped some of the mud off her face. 'I'll take you back to your place,' he said. 'You can have a bath and wash your hair. Then we need to talk.'

She could not hide her excitement. She gave a quick laugh and instructed Mike to complete the work in the garden. He looked sour. 'Thanks,' he said. 'On a bloody Sunday too. I have got a family, you know.'

'One of the joys of being a copper,' she said, then glanced up at the window and saw Evelyn's silhouette. 'Have a word with her, Mike,' she said. 'Tell her again. Ben is dead. Marilyn is dead. If she knows anything else she has a duty to tell us or she could be had up for wasting police time... withholding information... obstruction... And tell her we still want to get in touch with her husband. Tell her we're worried about her safety.' She stopped. 'Tell her she must tell us anything she knows.'

She paused. 'And tell her this. It'll be the house next, tell her. And, Mike,' she added, ignoring the look of disapproval on his face, 'tell her if she hears a dog it's someone else's animal. It's not Ben.'

Mike looked even more angry. 'So you're swanning off with him?'

Matthew was standing a short distance away, watching her patiently but with a look of amusement on his face. She knew exactly what he was thinking.

'We'll probably end up at the morgue,' she said, 'after I've had a bath.'

He shrugged his shoulders and turned away.

Matthew laid sheets of newspaper on the passenger seat and she got in and fastened her seat belt. He watched her quietly for a moment before starting the engine, smiled and moved away. As they swung into the traffic he briefly touched her hand. 'I can't tell you how good it is to see you in the car again.'

She didn't trust herself to speak.

She left Matthew downstairs, sitting relaxed on the sofa. He had always felt comfortable in the small cottage. She climbed the stairs, stripped and showered, shampooed her hair and wrapped a white towelling bathrobe around her. It was warm and comfortable in the sitting room. Matthew had opened a bottle of wine.

He grinned and raised his glass to her. 'That looks a bit better,' he said. 'Mucky work, digging the garden. And if you want my opinion,' he said, 'you were wasting your time – especially with my latest bit of information.'

She looked at him. 'A lot of police time is wasted,' she said defensively, 'following leads that take you nowhere. It doesn't matter as long as you reach the truth in the end.'

He studied her face. 'And you think you will?'

'Yes,' she said, but it was with a degree of uncertainty.

He paused and she waited for him to tell her, knowing he liked to be precise about forensic facts.

'I haven't redone the PM – yet,' he said cautiously, 'but I think I know how she died.'

She was sitting on the floor, in front of the fire, her hair spread out to dry. She ran her fingers through it, feeling it spring back as the dampness steamed away. She put her arms around her knees, looked up at Matthew sitting in the chair. He had switched on the standard lamp behind him, and the light touched his hair, giving it a yellow look. She listened as he spoke slowly, choosing his words as carefully as if he was in a court of law.

'Jo,' he said, watching her very carefully and she knew she was being tested. 'How much have you learned about Marilyn?'

She was surprised. He used the name with such familiarity. It disturbed her. She drank some of the wine, frowning.

'We know she blackmailed many people,' she said cautiously. 'We don't exactly know who yet but it seems quite a few people are involved.' She looked up. 'She knew things about people ... possibly her employer, Dr Wilson, we think Machin, the antique dealer. The next door neighbour seems absolutely terrified of her and we're curious about exactly what her connections were with Paul Haddon, the undertaker. It seems ...' she took a large swig of the wine, 'it seems he came to see her at the surgery fairly regularly.' She looked at Matthew. 'That's a long list of suspects, Mat.'

She drank again, frowned. 'Her bank accounts show large deposits but apart from her wages they were all cash so, although we know there was this huge disparity between her legitimate income and her outgoings, it's a little difficult to prove. Besides, Matthew, I don't really want to dig up everyone's little secret. I simply want to find out who killed her. The why doesn't matter so much. But to find out who killed her I first have to know how she died.'

She looked him square in the face, reading some uncertainty there. 'How well did you know her?'

'I knew her,' he said. 'She was a witch.'

And now she knew real, cold fear. She couldn't look at Matthew's face. All the time she had worried about his connection with the dead nurse. Now she knew she must face it to progress with the case.

'Go on,' she prompted.

'Jo,' he said softly, 'can I trust you? Which comes first – the person or the job?'

Now she knew she would be compromised. And as she watched his face very carefully she felt closer to him than she had ever felt before – closer now than when they had been lovers.

She spoke very softly. 'You can trust me, Matthew.'

'Let me tell you about her,' he said. 'You should know what sort of woman she was – whose murder you're investigating.'

'Was she blackmailing you too?'

He nodded. 'She tried.'

She was suddenly appalled. 'About me?'

Again he nodded. 'I told her to go to hell – do her damnedest!'

He leaned down and touched her hand. 'Do you remember that night, at the restaurant?'

'When Jane turned up?'

He nodded, drank a little of the wine and set it down on the coffee table. 'It was Marilyn who told Jane where we were. It was because I refused to pay her any money. I thought she was bluffing.'

She remembered the night – an intimate evening in a tiny hotel – a meal slowly tasted, quiet, shared conversation, giggles over numerous glasses of wine, a feeling that life was good, of warmth and comfort and good food, the promise of sex.

And then, shattering the peace of the restaurant like some hellish storm on a summer's sea, Jane had burst in, screaming and furious. Appalled and embarrassed, they had sprung to their feet, their quiet anonymity shattered. The other diners had watched with shocked eyes, knowing their secret, witnessing the noisy fury, as Jane spat out insults. 'Scarlet mistress, filthy whore.' Even now Joanna felt hot at the memory of that night, of Matthew's fumbling excuses, his face suffused with shame. He had left with Jane. She had paid the bill.

Two days later he had rung her and apologized and she had said what she knew he was thinking, that they should not meet again. A slow hatred of Marilyn Smith filled her. She closed her eyes and pictured the plump figure with her obscene greasy red lips, legs splayed . . . that picture of a dirty invitation.

She looked at Matthew. 'Her,' she said.

She refilled her glass, felt her face twist in sourness, drank it all. The good French wine tasted like vinegar.

Matthew was watching her. 'Now do you understand?'

She shook her head. 'It wasn't you, Matthew?' She gripped his arm. 'Tell me it wasn't you.'

He shook his head, gave a vague smile. 'No,' he said. 'Of course I didn't kill her. I couldn't stand her, but I wouldn't have killed her, Jo.'

'Then who?' she asked.

But he shook his head. 'Jo,' he said. 'That's for you to find out. I can tell you how. But I don't know who.'

'How will do for now, Matthew,' she said quietly and watched him pull a pale blue magazine from his pocket. '*British Medical Journal*,' he said. 'A couple of months ago.' He frowned. 'It suddenly came to me late last night. I remembered this article.' He flicked through the thin pages until he found the article and then pushed the magazine across to her. She glanced at it, read it, and looked at him for explanation.

'It actually happened,' he said awkwardly, 'in Canada, last year.'

She frowned. 'I don't understand.'

He glanced again at the magazine. 'An injection of insulin,' he said, 'well disguised. In this case in the crease underneath the breast. As the pathologist says in this article, she was a plump woman and it was tricky to find, but look.' He jabbed his finger on the photograph at the bottom of the page. 'He found it with a magnifying glass.' He looked at Joanna. 'There was so little to find: a slight swelling, a tiny bit of bruising . . . They could only confirm it by taking a biopsy of the surrounding tissues.' He paused. 'They were saturated with insulin.'

He looked carefully at Joanna. 'I bet there's a syringe mark somewhere on Marilyn Smith's body.'

'Surely you would have seen it, Matthew?'

He shook his head. 'Not necessarily.' He paused to think. 'I could have missed it.' His green eyes looked straight at her. 'Anyone could have missed it, Jo. We're talking about something very tiny – almost microscopic. Apart from obvious signs of homicide I was searching for a natural cause of death, and after that poisoning, maybe suicide. And suicide marks are easy to spot. The syringe would be there, dropped on the floor or lying on the bed with the phial. The mark would almost always be in the

147

arm. Sometimes they use the leg – but rarely. The mark we'll be looking for will be hidden ... folds of skin, between digits, even behind the hairline. It was only when I recalled the article that it all fell into place.' He looked at her. 'Do you remember me mentioning that she was sweaty?'

She nodded. 'Yes.'

'Insulin could cause that.' He stopped for a minute, frowning in concentration. 'Also the way she simply slipped into unconsciousness and died. There was no sign of a struggle, was there?'

She shook her head.

'It would all fit so neatly,' Matthew said. 'I should really have thought of it before. You see, the poisons lab wouldn't have found anything abnormal. Insulin is a naturally occurring substance. They wouldn't have looked for it.'

But Joanna shook her head. 'It won't work,' she said. 'She wouldn't have just lain there and let someone inject insulin into her.'

'She was zonked out,' Matthew said, 'or at the very least beautifully sleepy. Champagne, remember, a couple of sleeping tablets, new sexy underwear, lie back and think of England.'

'Matthew ... Why would she have taken sleeping tablets if she was expecting a night of passion?' She stopped. 'You don't think the capsules ...'

'I've always thought this,' he said. 'Easy to split a capsule.'

He waved his hands in the air. 'You can put rat poison in a capsule. What was actually in the capsule was a meticulously measured dose of phenobarbitone. I had the analysis back today. The lab rang up and asked if she had been epileptic. I rang Sammy Bose. No, she wasn't. But they'd found traces of phenobarbitone in her blood. Not enough to kill her, but enough to make her drowsy. A therapeutic dose, had she been an epileptic – but she wasn't.'

'But why take it?' she said. 'And where did that one different-coloured capsule come from?'

He sighed. 'Far be it from me to try to tell you your job,' he said. 'And anyway, it's only a guess. But I wondered if she was under the impression that it was an aphrodisiac.' He stopped. 'Remember I knew her. Not well, but she was amazingly gullible. And she believed in fantasies. It would have been in character for Marilyn to trust someone who sent her a capsule saying it was an aphrodisiac.'

'And yet she blackmailed all these people?'

'It wouldn't have worked anywhere but in a small, isolated moorlands town,' Matthew said grimly. 'People here care very much about their reputation. Anywhere else and they would have told her to get stuffed.'

She looked up at him. 'So she really was waiting for a lover – or thought she was. But it was an appointment with someone quite different.'

He nodded. 'I think so.'

'And that lover was no lover,' she said. 'They never had intercourse.'

He waited.

'He killed her.' She closed her eyes and pictured the scene – suddenly vivid and cruel. 'She lay there, zonked out, dressed up in the . . . black lace . . . waiting for someone. And he came and murdered her.'

'She wouldn't have known much about it. She died happy.'

'Did she, Matthew?'

He looked uneasy.

'Have you had another look at the body yet?' she asked.

'No,' he said. 'I've been in London. Besides,' he added, 'I thought it would be nice if you were there too.' He hesitated awkwardly. 'It's your first case as an inspector. And I did withhold information. I should have said I knew her, Jo.'

She looked anxious. 'I'm sort of hoping it isn't important.'

He bent forward and gave her a chaste kiss on the cheek. 'Put some clothes on,' he said. 'We'll go and have a look now.'

She was upstairs getting dressed when she heard the telephone ring. She cursed as Matthew answered it – cursed even louder when she heard him say, 'She's upstairs getting dressed.' Pulling on a sweater, she picked up the upstairs telephone.

Mike sounded even more grumpy than before. 'I thought you ought to know, ma'am,' he said sarcastically, 'we've found a man's overcoat buried in the garden.'

She wriggled her arms down the sleeves, the phone tucked underneath her chin. 'Where?'

'Near the french windows. It had been there a good few years,' he added. 'We've bagged it up – sent it off to forensics.'

'I don't suppose there was a name in it?'

'No.'

'Right.' She paused. 'You've finished there now?'

'I'm ringing from the station. The others have all buggered off home. I'm just about to go. Just thought I'd ring – see how you were getting on.' His voice was heavy with disapproval.

'I'm on my way down the morgue,' she said. 'Dr Levin thinks he may have a cause of death.'

Mike grunted.

'I'll see you in the morning, Mike.'

Matthew was waiting at the foot of the stairs.

'I wish you hadn't picked up the phone,' she snapped.

He looked injured. 'We weren't doing anything.'

She flushed and he grinned, looking mischievous and quite at ease.

'Tarzan jealous, is he?'

'Oh, shut up,' she said, suddenly angry with the pair of them. 'Let's get going to the bloody morgue.'

# Chapter 13

She was silent as they slipped on green gowns, gloves and masks. The porter wheeled in the trolley and she steeled herself for the ordeal.

Matthew shot her an enquiring look. 'Are you going to be all right, Jo?'

She smiled. 'I'll be fine, Mat,' she said. But she was dreading this. Post-mortems are not pretty and Marilyn Smith had been dead for almost a week.

He patted her shoulder. 'Sorry,' he said. 'I've rather dragged you down here, haven't I?'

'Where else should I be?' she said stoutly. 'I'm the investigating officer. I belong here. If it's murder I want to know who.'

He gave her a warm grin and said nothing. He pulled back the sheet on the mottled corpse and stared down for a moment. 'She must have died,' he said, 'thinking of promises and hopes, dreaming in perfume and champagne, clouded with phenobarbitone.'

'I wonder,' she said, trying to suppress the feeling of nausea and revulsion.

He blinked.

'Is it murder, Matthew? Because if it was,' she said, 'killers can kill again. And clever killers can kill again – cleverly.'

Scarred by the pathologist's knife and hacksaw, minus viscera and hastily sewn back together, Marilyn Smith was indeed not a pretty sight.

Joanna felt both sick and faint. She leaned against the wall. 'It doesn't get any easier,' she said.

Matthew laughed and handed her a huge magnifying glass.

'Keep busy,' he said. 'That's the secret. Help me look. Forget she was human and think of her as a scientific exercise. Concentrate on the less obvious places: folds of skin, between the toes, underneath the breasts. Remember the article.'

And looking at the discoloured lump of meat it was easy to believe this thing had never been alive, a thinking, doing, moving person. A spiteful person who had harmed many people's lives. Joanna glanced across at Matthew and knew Marilyn had harmed them. They had not seen each other since that night in the restaurant.

The faintness threatened to engulf her again and she felt herself falling. But his hands were on her shoulders.

'Jo. It's a good job I'm a sympathetic pathologist.' He looked at her good humouredly. 'What the macho members of the force would make of this strong urge to pass out I don't know.' He tutted. 'What the hell would Tarzan say?'

She laughed. 'Please, Matthew,' she said. 'Leave him out of this.' Then she remembered the telephone call and started to giggle. 'What must he have thought?'

Matthew's eyes were warm as he watched her. He raised his eyebrows and said nothing.

She concentrated on the job.

'Behind the ear,' he said, 'in the hairline, feel for lumps and bumps . . . between the fingers, in creases.'

'You've cobbled her up a bit crudely.'

'I'm not Harley Street,' he said. 'This woman is never going to sue and, what's more, Jo, she'll never complain again. These incisions would never have healed, however skilfully I'd drawn them together.'

Joanna swallowed. 'I think I'm going to be sick,' she said.

152

Matthew was unsympathetic. 'Then go out.'

She looked helplessly at him, then suddenly vomited into the basin. 'I'll never get used to PMs,' she complained when she had finished, and washed her face in cold water. 'The stink of disinfectant.' She looked up. 'I think it's that that makes me feel so sick. Can't they put a different perfume—'

'I've found it,' Matthew said quietly, 'classic medical school hiding place: between the toes, syringe inserted towards the ball of the foot.' He straightened up. 'Clever,' he said. 'Very clever.' He moved the magnifying glass closer to Marilyn's right foot, adjusted the light to beam down on a tiny puncture wound, still crusted with a pinprick of blood, between the second and third toe. Now they concentrated on it, the ball of the foot was slightly swollen.

'Clever,' he muttered again, 'very very clever.' He crossed the room and brought back a camera with tripod, adjusted the lens. Then he looked at Joanna. 'Would you mind holding the toes apart?' he asked. 'And just drape this green towel behind it – it makes a good backcloth,' he explained.

She stood there while he clicked the shutter, conflicts of emotion moving across her face like stormy weather across the sky. She had been right all the time. It had been murder. Thoughts tumbled through her mind.

'Matthew,' she said softly. 'Medical knowledge? Access to drugs, someone who had read the article? Someone who could get hold of a syringe?'

'It wouldn't be that difficult.'

'There was no syringe found in the room,' she said. 'And Marilyn didn't inject her own feet.'

She met Matthew's serious gaze. 'It was murder,' she said quietly. 'She was murdered.'

He nodded. 'That's right.'

She watched as Matthew fished a scalpel from a drawer and cut tissue from around the puncture wound. 'If I'm right,' he said, dropping it into a specimen pot, 'this will be saturated with human insulin. I'll have to ring the coroner's office.'

She sat down in the corner of the room and drew out her notebook. The field was narrowed . . . Evelyn . . . Did this let her off the hook?

Jonah Wilson . . . She sat and pondered the quietly spoken doctor. Somehow she did not see him leading Marilyn on, suggesting an aphrodisiac, quietly sneaking in and murdering her. But he did fit the bill. A married man. Daily contact with his nurse, and she had been obsessed with him. And yet . . . She shook her head. No, he was not the killer.

Paul Haddon . . .? She looked at Matthew. 'How much medical knowledge does an undertaker have?'

He shrugged his shoulders. 'Difficult to say. The basics . . .' He met her eyes. 'Paul is an old friend of mine,' he said slowly.

'The whole bloody suspect list seem to be "old friends" of yours, Matthew,' she said sarcastically.

He flushed. 'Perhaps I should have told you. I was at medical school with Paul and Jonah, although Paul left after the first year.'

She waited.

'He was thrown out,' he said.

She stared at him.

'All rumours,' he said uncomfortably. 'Something happened one day in the dissection room.'

'What?'

'Oh, God . . .' Matthew ran his fingers through his hair. 'I don't know,' he said. 'Not for sure.'

'What?' she demanded.

'Someone said . . .' He dragged the words out. 'He'd been masturbating in there.'

She felt sick. 'And you said nothing when he set up as an undertaker?'

Matthew was silent.

'By God, Matthew,' she said. 'Your loyalty to your friends is touching.' She paused to think for a while. 'So

154

Paul Haddon has peculiar habits with the dead,' she said, 'as well as having the basics of medical knowledge. Is that right?'

He looked miserable. 'Lots of people know about insulin.'

'But not many people have access to insulin,' she pointed out. 'And how many would have read the article?'

'They wouldn't have to have read it,' he objected.

'No, but it's a sort of manual of how to kill someone and get away with it. Matthew, it even gave the dosage.'

He shrugged his shoulders. 'Look, Jo,' he said awkwardly. 'Please. Don't expect me to start pointing fingers. I've told you how. It's as much as I know – honestly. I don't know who.'

She pressed her lips together. 'I've always thought it funny,' she said slowly, 'how many of the wrong people use that word – honestly.'

She sat still, watching Matthew cleaning up with the mortuary attendant, and filling in the forms.

She glanced at her watch. It was ten o'clock.

He crossed the floor towards her. 'Come on, Jo,' he said. 'You look done in. I'll buy you a drink.'

But she shook her head. 'Go home, Matthew. Go home to your wife and daughter.'

And she walked out and left him.

'Sit down, Piercy.'

Superintendent Arthur Colclough looked quite friendly this morning in spite of the working weekend. His face grew even brighter when she related the results of last night's forage in the mortuary.

'Clever,' he said softly. 'Bloody killers. They're getting smarter every day.'

She watched him warily.

'Think you can handle it?'

She nodded. 'I'll get back to you, Sir, if we're getting nowhere.'

His eyes gleamed. 'Following a number of leads?'

'Yes.'

He stood up then. 'Well, Piercy. Mustn't keep you from your work, must I?'

'Mike . . .' She called him into her office. 'Sit down,' she said, and she filled him in with the results of last night's investigation.

'So you were right,' he said. 'Murder.' Then he voiced the thought that had kept her awake all night. 'I suppose it must have been Jonah Wilson.'

She looked unhappily at him. 'He's top of the list,' she said.

Mike frowned. 'There's no one else on the list, is there? I can't really imagine Evelyn Shiers doing it.'

'One thing,' she said. 'Haddon did the first year at medical school, then he left.' She shrugged her shoulders and was conscious she had said nothing about Matthew's connection with the dead woman.

'See if you can get in touch with the dean of the medical school,' she said. 'Get some details about Haddon.'

'And what about the overcoat?'

'Let's have a look.'

The coat had been a good one – Burberry, grey gaberdine. Now it was a rotted rag. It smelled musty, earthy. Joanna picked it up and searched in one pocket. Empty. She tried the other one and pulled out a latch key. She glanced at Mike. 'Did it fit Mrs Shiers' door?'

Mike mumbled his reply. 'Missed that somehow.'

She handed it to him. 'Go back,' she said. 'Better try it. And, Mike,' she added. 'Ask Mrs Shiers if she's ever done any nursing.'

Mike looked meaningfully at her. 'Well done. You stuck at it. Good for you. I suppose I can be glad I didn't bet more than ten pounds on it.'

She smiled then. 'I'm a cautious better, Mike,' she said. 'It hasn't cost you much.' She waited a minute, then stood up and stared out of the window. 'And I promise you it gives me no feeling of satisfaction. She was a bitch of a woman.' A tight feeling of anger suddenly touched her as she felt again the hot embarrassment of the night in the hotel. 'If it was Dr Wilson,' she said quietly, 'he was a better person than she.'

She paused again. Then, 'Mike ... Undertakers use syringes for embalming, don't they?'

'So do drug addicts,' he said. 'Oh, hell. I nearly forgot. Talking about drug addicts, someone rang for you.'

'Who?'

He glanced at the message pad on the desk, by the telephone. 'Patty,' he said. 'Patty Brownlow.'

She looked blankly at him.

'Said she worked at the antique shop. Said she had some information.'

'Is Grenville Machin still under surveillance?'

'Yes.'

'Have you a number?'

He supplied it and she dialled but there was no reply. She put the phone down. 'Let's go and talk to Dr Wilson, shall we?'

Joanna glanced around the waiting room, at the rows of the old, the sick, the decrepit, the depressed ... all of whom depended on the doctor. And she was conscious of their curious gaze on the two police. Her thoughts reeled. How could one man shoulder such a burden and then go home to a sick wife? And in cold blood murder a woman who believed he was about to make love to her? It didn't fit.

She frowned at Mike. 'We're making a mistake,' she whispered. 'This isn't right. It can't be him.'

Mike cracked his knuckles loudly. The sound was like a pistol shot and several of the patients looked up sharply. He leaned towards her and whispered, 'Don't doubt yourself, ma'am. Let's just interview him. Softly softly.'

The buzzer sounded. Another patient stood up, hung

his number on a board, shuffled through the door towards the surgery.

Joanna looked at Mike. A baby was crying. 'Have you ever arrested a doctor?'

He grinned. 'Drunk driving,' he said.

They sat in silence for a few minutes. Then the surgery door opened. Jonah Wilson was walking towards them. She stared. He had changed almost beyond recognition.

He smiled at her with world-weary eyes, bloodshot through lack of sleep. 'Inspector,' he said with some relief. 'I think I'm glad to see you.'

'We won't keep you long, Dr Wilson,' she said. 'I know you have a lot of patients to see. Just a few questions.'

She waited until they were sitting in his consulting room before speaking. 'Marilyn was murdered,' she said bluntly, and waited for his reaction.

He looked bleakly at her, his shoulders bent, his body sagging. 'I thought she probably was,' he said.

As she watched him Joanna was struck by a thought. If he and Matthew had been in medical school together they must be around the same age. Jonah looked years older.

'Do you know why she was murdered?' he asked carefully.

She nodded. 'We believe she blackmailed people,' she said. 'We know large sums of money were paid into a building society account. Far more than she was earning here in the surgery.'

The doctor breathed out hard. 'Do you know who?' he said. 'Who she was blackmailing?'

'Several people,' Joanna said, then took a deep breath. 'She was blackmailing you, wasn't she, Doctor?'

She knew from his face. This was what he had been dreading. He swallowed hard. 'Yes,' he whispered.

Mike stepped forward. 'Would you like to tell us what she was blackmailing you about? Get it off your chest?'

Jonah's eyes dropped and he glanced evasively around

158

the surgery. 'It was a professional thing,' he said. 'A mistake with a patient.'

Joanna glanced at Mike. He gave a very slight shake of his head. They both knew Jonah Wilson was not telling the truth ... at least, not the whole truth. 'The patient died,' he said.

She waited. 'We'll want details, Doctor.'

Jonah nodded. 'Of course.'

'How did she find out about the mistake?' Mike asked casually.

'She spotted something in the notes.'

'Dr Wilson.' Mike's voice was hard and threatening. The doctor seemed to shrink. His eyes pleaded with Mike.

'It was you, wasn't it, who she was waiting for that night?'

Jonah Wilson jumped up. 'No!' he said. 'No. It wasn't me. I swear it.'

The worst thing was Joanna believed him. 'And that's all you can tell us?'

Jonah nodded.

She tried a different tack. 'What can you tell me about Paul Haddon?'

The doctor visibly dropped his guard. 'He's the undertaker,' he said.

'We know that.' Mike's voice was hostile.

'He's good at his job.'

'He came in to see Marilyn frequently.'

'I didn't know that.'

'Was there anything between them?'

This time the doctor was certain. 'No,' he said. 'No. I'm sure of it. There wasn't.' He paused. 'In fact, I don't think they liked each other very much.'

'What made you think that?'

'I don't know ... I don't know.'

There was a long silence, then Jonah Wilson asked timidly, 'How ... how did she die?'

Joanna looked at him. He was shaking. 'We think she

159

probably died of an insulin overdose. We're waiting for some results from the lab.'

The doctor looked up. 'But . . .' he began.

'Deliberately administered.' Mike's voice was much harder than hers. She saw the doctor turn back to her as something like terror moved in his eyes.

'God – no,' he said. 'No.' Then he shuddered. 'How horrible.'

'You keep insulin here, in the surgery?'

Joanna could hear the accusation in Mike's voice.

'Yes. I think you would find most doctors keep a supply of insulin. It's used quite commonly for diabetic comas.'

'Where do you keep it?'

'Some in the fridge. A few phials in my bag.' He looked from one to the other, then dropped his head in his hands. 'This is a nightmare,' he muttered.

'Is there anything else you want to say, Doctor?' Mike spoke very quietly. 'Perhaps down at the police station?'

Jonah Wilson stared at him. 'No,' he said. 'Please. Who would look after Pamella?'

Joanna started. For a moment she had forgotten about Pamella, and now she suddenly knew Pamella was important.

The doctor blew out a quick breath of air as though he could not hold it any longer. 'Lots of people might have wanted to murder a nurse,' he said, 'if she was using information about her patients to extract money from them. It would be extortion,' he said. 'Surely that would be a reason for wanting to kill her.'

'The person we're looking for,' Mike said harshly, 'wanted to kill her. But he pretended he wanted to make love to her.'

The doctor went white.

'Oh yes. Plenty of people might have wanted to kill her. But wanting to make love. It narrows the field, doesn't it?'

Joanna glanced around the room. Sure enough there

was a pile of *British Medical Journals*. She met Mike's eyes and knew he had seen them too.

'And the night call that you went on was round about eleven o'clock?'

Jonah Wilson couldn't fail to pick up the accusation in Mike's voice. 'There was a night call and I did go. You can check up.'

'We already have,' Mike said.

Joanna rose to leave. 'We'll find out who killed her, Doctor. It'll all come out in the end.' She hesitated, then asked a final question. 'Were you the reason Marilyn Smith bought those new undergarments, Doctor?' she asked. 'Was she hoping to entice you to her bed?'

Jonah flushed. 'No,' he said. 'No. I swear it. I love my wife,' he said sincerely. 'I never found Marilyn attractive. I had my chance,' he said.

'Really?' Mike's eyes held steady.

'Oh . . .' Jonah looked as though he wished he had not spoken. 'She had a bit of a thing about me, years ago. It was nothing. I married Pamella.' He scratched his head. 'I've never regretted it, even though my wife is sick. To be frank,' he said, 'Marilyn revolted me.' His eyes were filled with shame and Joanna knew Marilyn would have made this shy man's life a misery.

He looked at Joanna with a pleading expression in his eyes. 'What can I do to convince you?'

'You don't have to, for the moment,' she said, and rose to leave. 'But I don't want you to take any trips out of the area, Dr Wilson.' We'll need you in for further questioning.'

The doctor nodded with a glimmer of dry humour. 'I understand, Inspector,' he said. 'Don't leave town.'

They left the surgery little wiser.

Mike attempted an encouraging grin. 'So far so good,' he said.

'But what do you think, Mike?'

He rubbed the back of his neck in an awkward gesture. 'I don't know,' he said. 'I'm like you. The facts fit. Everything fits except him. I can't see him killing someone. He isn't the type.'

'They can't all fit into some psychologist's profile,' she said. 'We'll have to shake that one off. He has to have done it. Who else?'

Something triggered a picture in her mind: long, bony white fingers touching dead flesh, unnaturally pale skin, a thin gash of a mouth, a faintly lascivious look in the dark eyes. On impulse she touched Mike's arm. 'Come with me,' she said.

'Where?'

'The funeral parlour.'

Four gleaming black limousines stood outside, parked side by side. All were empty, including the hearse. Joanna approached the glazed door with a feeling of sick apprehension, even though Mike was near enough to touch. They said nothing but crept nearer the door.

It was still inside, and empty. They moved in without knocking, creeping across the thick carpet towards the chapel of rest, towards a just perceptible sound – a rhythmic, animal grunting . . .

What was it the dean of the medical school had said . . .? 'An indecent act with his allocated body.' With a feeling of sick horror she knew what she would find inside and looked helplessly at Mike. From his face she knew the thought had not crossed his mind. But he didn't know all that she knew.

The door into the chapel was thick oak, with twin panels of bottle glass through which she could see a dark shape moving up and down . . . up and down. As they listened they heard him cry out and groan. And then they pushed open the door.

He stood up, grey and sick-looking, his wet, pink, obscene object the only splash of colour in the room apart from the bright colours of spring bouquets set around the chapel, flowers of mourning.

'Oh, God . . .' Mike's face was white with shock as he

found himself staring at a wax-faced corpse.

Paul Haddon struggled with his trousers. Eyes starting out of his head, he began to jibber and as quickly sank down on the steps in front of the altar and collapsed in high-pitched, hysterical sobs.

# Chapter 14

The telephone was ringing as she walked into her office but when she picked it up the name meant nothing to her. Yesterday's events still crowded her mind.

'Patty Brownlow,' the voice said again. 'I work at the antique shop.'

'I'm sorry.' Joanna apologized. 'I do remember. What can I do for you?' She mouthed the girl's name to Mike through the open door.

'It isn't what you can do for me . . .' The girl sounded irritated.

'Then what . . .?'

'It's what I can do for you. Listen, I'm not coming down the nick. He'd find out, but I can help you nail him.'

Mike was by her side, breathing down her neck, trying to listen.

'Is it about the nurse?'

'No . . .' the girl said impatiently. 'He knew her all right. Paid her money, too. In fact he'd have liked to have got his hands around her bloody neck. You know all that stuff round at her house? She never paid a bean for it. Just waltzed in . . . took her pick.'

'Why?'

'She found out things . . . things she'd no business knowing.'

'How did she find out?'

'Maybe I'll tell you, maybe not, but she knew plenty about old Gren. She had enough to pop him in a cage

164

for the rest of his life. Did you know she'd been to Spain?'

Joanna shook her head. 'No, but what's that got to do with . . .'

'The doll . . .' Mike was hissing in her ear. 'The flamenco doll. In the bedroom,' he added.

Joanna recalled it, standing more than three feet high, back bent, arms outflung, frilled dress, shocking pink, black mantilla. She nodded. 'Patty,' she said, 'what's Spain got to do with it?'

'Tell you later,' the girl said softly, and, after a pause, 'Look, do you want what I can give you or not?'

Joanna sighed. She didn't want to be sidetracked. Not now when she was so close. 'I'm investigating a murder.'

Mike scowled, his jaw set. His great ham fist was clenched. Joanna knew he would have liked to bring it slamming down on to the desk. 'For God's sake,' he said through clenched teeth.

'I don't know anything about that.' The girl was uncompromising. 'But I do know this. He didn't kill her.'

'How do you know?'

''Cause I was bloody well with him all that night.'

'So what have you got for me?' Joanna asked wearily.

The girl was scornful. 'Don't you coppers ever want to nick anyone these days? Haven't you even noticed someone's helping themselves to every bloody Doulton figure within a thirty-mile radius? Don't you understand crack and heroin are cheaper here than in bloody Colombia?'

Now Joanna knew she could not afford to ignore Patty's information. 'Exactly what do you know?' she asked coldly.

The girl gave a dry laugh. 'The bloody lot,' she said.

In his anxiety to hear Mike was leaning on her. Joanna shifted irritably and listened to Patty's scornful voice.

'Don't tell me you didn't know it was him all along?'

Mike let out his breath in a slow, satisfied gasp.

'Listen, I rang up to say this. You'll have to move fast. Unloading's tonight. If you don't catch him I don't know when the next lot's due. And, it won't be at the warehouse. Try Good Cow Farm . . . the barns around the back.'

'Patty. He's your boyfriend. Why are you doing this?'

'Well . . . that's my business, not yours. I have my reasons.' She paused, then added, 'Don't cock it up, will you? He's getting more and more devious. It'll be some time after midnight. All right?'

The phone went dead and Joanna met Mike's eyes.

He couldn't conceal his delight. 'Bloody marvellous,' he said, rubbing his hands together. 'Bloody brilliant.'

'Look . . .' she said awkwardly. 'I am in the middle of a murder investigation . . .'

'Joanna. You can't ignore a hint like this. You just can't.'

She rubbed her forehead. 'Mike,' she said, 'I'm nearly ready to bring the whole thing to a close. The inquest is in two days' time. I've got reports to write.' She grinned. 'It's all right, Mike,' she said. 'I'm only winding you up. Let's get things sorted out for tonight, shall we? There's a lot to do.'

It was a chilly night with a steady drizzle. Good Cow Farm was on a quiet road in the low end of the moorlands. Access was along narrow farm tracks. And that made it easy – except for the officers who had to approach the farm across the fields at the back.

Joanna and Mike walked together through the fields. She sensed his excitement as they approached the two huge Dutch barns.

'I thought this place was derelict,' he whispered. 'A family lived here three or four years ago. They all died except the old lady. She went to live with a daughter.'

'Who farms it?'

Mike shrugged. 'Neighbours.' He looked at the deserted yard. 'It looks damned quiet here,' he said. 'You don't think she's played a trick on us, do you?'

Joanna shivered. 'Who knows? I'm bloody freezing.'

She paused. 'No, I don't think she's played a trick. She sounded genuine.'

They were silent for a minute then Mike whispered again.

'It wouldn't be the first time we've been led out on a wild goose chase. What time did she say?'

'After midnight.'

Joanna spoke quietly into her walkie talkie. 'All quiet ...?'

A crackle and then the affirmative. They settled down to wait.

All along the approach roads police cars crouched, hidden behind hedges, up drives ... More than forty men were deployed around the area. Joanna blew on her hands and wished she was sitting in one of the cars. Why the hell did she always feel she had to be out there – one of the boys?

Close by, an owl hooted and a fox barked. Out in the gloom she could hear the distant barking of a dog. It reminded her of Ben. Even farther away, the distant whine of the traffic. A pale halo of soft pink lit the sky in the direction of the town. She felt on the very edge of the world.

Mike cleared his throat. 'How long are we going to give it?'

She smiled at his impatience. 'All night, Mike,' she whispered back.

She could see his face white against the side of the barn. Police should learn from gangsters, she thought. Dress for the occasion ... black balaclavas and gloves. She turned on Mike. 'Not getting cold feet, are you, Sergeant?'

He fell silent and she squatted down against the side of the barn, wrapping her coat around her. The damp penetrated her bones and she wished she'd worn another sweater. She closed her eyes, tried to distract her mind from the dripping gutters and the cold. Something niggled. Something was wrong.

Start at the beginning...

Marilyn lying dead. Black lace and boned, a plump figure pinched into shapeliness. The house untouched... A capsule... champagne... perfume... music. The Spanish doll.

She opened her eyes. Jonah, Matthew, Paul Haddon starting medical school together... and Paul had had to go. But Matthew and Jonah must have known each other very well. Must have been friends for many years. They would have stuck together, through thick and thin.

Pamella and Marilyn... Pamella the pretty one, Marilyn having the cast-offs when her friend had finished with them. Until Jonah... She had formed a conviction that one day she would inherit Jonah too. But it wasn't to be. He had never come – or had he?

Pamella's illness... sparked off by the birth of the first baby, Stevie. What had really happened to Stevie? He had died. And the label – cot death – now seemed too convenient. Matthew would have done the post-mortem...

A cold trickle of fear ran down her neck. Matthew was a pathologist. Pamella had been ill. The baby had died. Marilyn Smith would have had access to the notes. Matthew and Jonah were old friends. They would have stuck together. The more she rolled the facts around her mind the less she liked them and she knew now. She had to speak to Matthew.

She felt a jab in her ribs.

'Have a swig.' Mike handed her a small flask of spirits. 'Hope you like whisky,' he said.

She downed one small, sour mouthful and handed it back.

He stood up briskly. 'Here we go...' Exultation made his voice quick and gruff. 'They're here, Patty my girl...'

Joanna put a hand on his arm. 'Steady, Mike,' she warned. 'We aren't home and dry yet, you know.'

Wide arcs of lights turned swiftly along the track that led to Good Cow farm.

Mike clutched her arm. 'We'll get him, Joanna,' he said. 'In the bloody bag.' She saw his teeth gleam white as he grinned, then they ducked behind one of the plastic-covered rolls of hay.

'Let them start unloading,' she'd instructed the force. 'Give them some time. Watch and write the whole lot down. Use tape recorders if necessary. Videos, even. Then pounce.'

And for the first time in more than a week Joanna forgot about the dead nurse and enjoyed the high at the thought of Machin's face when they finally nicked him.

The lorries turned into the yard. Men climbed out. One lit a cigarette, tossed the match into a puddle.

'Leave the headlights on.'

It was Machin. The big fish had come to supervise. They could not have hoped for more. No slick denials of involvement this time.

Wide barn doors rolled open. The headlights picked up a pale smog and long-legged black figures moving efficiently, carrying tea chests – two to a man. They must be heavy. There was laughter and good-humoured banter ... 'Mind my toes ...' 'Stick it over there, Guv.'

'Room in the corner?' The men busied themselves like modern-day smugglers.

When it happened it happened fast.

The police cars swung in. Figures ran out. Joanna and Mike stood up.

'Shit.'

'The bloody fuzz.'

'Drop the damned ...'

It was over in minutes. Two figures tried to run and were felled by waiting police in the next field. Machin stood bemused in the middle of the courtyard. He glared at Joanna as she and Mike emerged from the shadows.

'Someone told you,' he accused. 'You didn't just happen to be here. Who told you?'

'I did, you bastard.'

Machin wheeled around. 'Patty. Patty?'

169

Joanna almost felt sorry for him.

He stared at the tiny figure in skintight jeans, fringed cowboy boots and a mock-leopardskin coat.

She climbed neatly out of the cab and planted herself in front of Machin. 'I shopped you, you bastard,' she said. 'I'm glad I did. Perhaps that'll pay you back.'

Machin looked astounded. 'Patty – love,' he held out his arms to her. 'What's going on?'

She grinned at him, hands on hips. 'I bet you wondered how that nurse knew so much about you,' she said. 'I'll tell you a little story, shall I? I expect you've got plenty of time. No more rushing around now. I think the police will want to detain you.

'A nurse from Leek went on a little holiday,' she said. 'And she met my sister who owns a bar out there. Remember Astrid Lucas, Gren?'

Machin made no response and she continued.

'My sister. And little Robbie just happens to be my favourite nephew. So when people start threatening him I get upset.'

Machin gazed at her for a long time before he recovered himself. When eventually he spoke his voice was firm and threatening.

'Don't go to sleep at night, Patty, my little humming bird,' he said softly. ''Cause one night you'll wake up and I'll be standing there. And I won't have a bloody Durex in my hand neither.'

She gave a short laugh. 'You won't be standing anywhere near me, Gren, for a very long time.' She put her face close to his. 'When you do stand near me, my dear, you'll need a zimmerframe to hold you up.' She let out another peal of laughter and turned to the watching police. 'Like my wit?'

No one answered. There was something both brave and pathetic about the tiny figure. Joanna feared for her safety. People like Patty Brownlow were vulnerable. Machin's net would spread wide.

Mike cautioned the six men they had rounded up and

Joanna levered the top off one of the crates. As expected, they were full of china figures.

'Inspector . . .' One of the uniformed boys was shining his torch in the cab of the second lorry. She peered inside and wondered that anyone could possibly be so careless. Under the seat were stored plastic carrier bags containing the catch she had hoped for. Heroin, resembling poor-quality Demerara sugar, packed in plastic bags . . . pounds of it.

Now she permitted herself to smile at Mike.

'Got him,' she said.

# Chapter 15

She watched Matthew take the stand at the inquest and give his evidence.

'On further examination I discovered a hypodermic mark on the deceased's right foot between the second and third digit.'

The coroner looked at him over half-moon spectacles. 'You had not noticed it at the first post-mortem, Dr Levin?'

'No, sir,' he said.

Mike leaned across. 'He missed it first time. Might have helped us a bit if he'd got on to it a bit quicker.'

She scowled at him.

'And when you found it, what did you infer from the hypodermic mark, Doctor?'

'I believed Marilyn Smith had been administered an injection.'

The coroner raised his eyebrows.

'I took a biopsy from around the injection site and on analysis the sample was discovered to contain abnormal amounts of insulin.'

The coroner cleared his throat. 'Interesting...' he mused. 'Don't think I've ever come across this one before.'

Mike dug her in the ribs. 'Joanna,' he said. 'Look who's here.'

She turned round and met the blackcurrant eyes of Marilyn's mother. She frowned. 'Vivian Smith's travelled all this way?' She met Mike's eyes. 'I wonder why,' she said. 'She doesn't pretend there was much love lost between them.'

She turned round again. Mrs Smith was staring at her as though she wanted to speak. She nodded and turned back to Matthew.

He had almost finished giving evidence ... blood insulin levels, time of death ... Absence of indication of sexual intercourse. Neatly he concentrated on the facts. Joanna had watched him countless times in court give such evidence. It always sounded truthful – plausible. But she had heard Matthew sound just as plausible on the telephone to his wife, telling her he would be working late – again. His chin jutted out, he was sure of himself, confident. The expert pathologist.

But now it was her turn.

Her evidence was routine. Referring after each question to her notes, Joanna briefly described what she had found at Silk Street.

The coroner peered at her. 'What were your initial thoughts, Inspector Piercy?'

She started. This was unusual. Coroners generally dealt in facts not opinions, and Konrad Fowler was particularly fond of reminding her of that.

'I simply want to know who died, when and, wherever possible, how, Inspector. No need for you to make a drama out of events.'

From the witness box she met his eyes and he gave a slight, acknowledging smile. 'Carry on,' he said.

She cleared her throat. 'At that time,' she said, 'I was unsure. There seemed no obvious cause of death ...'

The coroner finished the sentence for her and addressed the court. 'In the absence of a syringe or indeed an obvious source of insulin – the deceased not being a diabetic or in receipt of this particular drug – I have no option but to find the cause of death as being the result of unlawful killing.' He paused. 'This is indeed a most unusual method of disposal ...' He adjusted his glasses and extended sympathy to family and friends.

Vivian Smith sat bolt upright, unsmiling, staring at Joanna's back.

Matthew walked up to Joanna as soon as the verdict was announced. He gave a weak smile. 'Your first homicide.'

She yawned and tried to smother it. 'Sorry,' she said. 'I've been up most of the night.'

Matthew's eyes softened. 'So I heard. On the local news. You trawled in a haul of villains last night.'

She nodded. 'There'll be others,' she said, 'to take their place.' She hesitated for a moment then spoke without meeting his eyes. 'I'm going to have to ask you some more questions, Matthew,' she said. 'I'm not happy about your statement.'

He tensed and then sagged slightly. He looked tired, as old and bowed as Jonah Wilson. 'I see,' he said formally. 'I suppose I could have expected that. Well . . . as usual I'm all yours . . .' He hesitated for a moment then spoke again. 'You're creating havoc here in such a small town, Jo. Who will be next, I wonder?'

She watched him carefully. 'I wonder,' she echoed.

He moved closer. 'I heard another whisper,' he said. 'Paul Haddon.'

'We've tried to keep it quiet,' she said softly. 'How the hell do you know about that?'

'His mother rang,' he said, green eyes troubled and upset. 'He got home in such a state.'

'He was bloody lucky we let him go at all,' she said. 'Have you any idea what he gets up to in that place?'

He put a hand on her arm. 'Thank God I do not,' he said and she glared at him.

'Well, I bloody well walked in on him,' she said, 'and I don't think I'll ever forget the experience. Didn't you ever wonder about him, Matthew, after what you heard at college?'

'But I never knew for sure why he was ejected,' he reminded her.

'No,' she said, 'but you had an idea. You might have

kept an eye on him... He became an undertaker, for God's sake,' she said. 'After being disciplined for an act – with a corpse, for your information, Matthew. Mike rang the dean of the medical school. It was an obscene act with a body.'

'I didn't know for sure,' he said defensively.

'So you buried your head in the sand.'

'Will you be pressing charges?'

'I've filed a report to the CPS,' she said cautiously. 'It's up to them what they do with it.'

'It'll ruin him, you know.'

She was suddenly very angry. 'Matthew. Whose side are you on? The necrophiliac's? You can't be that sick.'

'God,' he said. 'St George had nothing on you charging around putting wrongs to rights.'

'Between you and me,' she said softly, glancing around the room, 'I don't think we will press charges. I don't want to see it get out. It would cause too much upset. Personally, I hope it will be hushed up and Haddon cautioned and forbidden from pursuing his particular career. We'll keep a watch on him,' she added.

'Here's to that,' he said, 'and to your long string of successes.'

She gave a wry smile.

'Excuse me...'

She hadn't noticed Vivian Smith approaching from behind.

'I'm sorry... Mrs Smith...'

Marilyn's mother pursed her lips. 'I thought you'd want to know... I thought you might be interested. I got a letter,' she said finally, pulling a brown envelope from her handbag. 'She always sent things second class, at least to me she did.' Her eyes became pinpoints. 'Mean, she was.'

Joanna eyed the envelope and invited Vivian Smith back to the station.

Once in her office she pulled on gloves and then slid the letter out of the envelope on to her desk. It was not long

– only half a page. It greeted her mother, mentioned the money enclosure, grumbled about one of the receptionists. And it enthused about the 'new boyfriend'... a married man... 'It's funny, Mother... how things turn out. And now I know. He's loved me all these years...'

It was the writing of a happy woman who had eventually found love. It turned Joanna's stomach. She glanced at the finishing sentences.

'So I went out, Ma... went absolutely wild... bought up the shop.'

And the last sentence was the most poignant of all. 'I'll send you more next month. I promise...' It was signed simply: Love... and a scrawled 'Marilyn'.

And for the first time Joanna felt a lump of grief for the death of the nurse. She looked up at Vivian Smith. 'Can you confirm it is her writing?'

Vivian Smith nodded.

Joanna handed the letter back to her. 'Thank you,' she said, then as Vivian Smith hesitated she added, 'There won't be any forensic evidence from this.'

Vivian Smith looked straight at her. 'I wasn't thinking about that,' she said. Her beady eyes looked hard. 'It was him – wasn't it? It was him who did her in?'

'We think so,' Joanna said cautiously.

Vivian Smith swallowed. 'It was murder,' she said, 'wasn't it?'

Joanna wondered whether Marilyn's mother was at last beginning to grieve for her daughter – but the next sentence dispensed that thought.

'When will I get her things? The house... the car...' she said greedily. 'They're all worth something. I'll have to sell them.'

Joanna was silent.

'Well, I don't want to live up here,' she said defensively. 'Cardiff's where I belong.'

# Chapter 16

It was a drive she had sometimes made in her imagination but nothing could have prepared her for the beauty of the old stone farmhouse where Matthew lived with his wife and ten-year-old daughter, Eloise.

They drove up the narrow, stony road bordered by fields of sheep and ranch-style fencing and Joanna watched with mounting tension. She felt sick. Her mouth was dry. For ten pence she would have asked Mike to turn the car round and drive back into Leek. But she didn't and they drove through a five-barred gate into a cobbled courtyard with barns in front and mounting steps to the side. On the top step sat a small black and white cat licking its paws and watching through narrow green eyes.

The house was built of warm mellow grey stone, covered with moss. And to Joanna's eyes on that late spring morning it looked like heaven. Daffodils swayed in a light, cool breeze, golden trumpets of the summer's dawn. She sat, mesmerized.

Mike dug her in the ribs. 'Do you want me to come in with you?'

She sighed and shook her head. 'No,' she said. 'I ought to go alone.'

'Don't compromise yourself . . .' Mike warned. He looked worried.

She opened the car door. 'I won't.' She smiled. 'It's all right, Mike,' she said. She hesitated. 'And I'll be some time. I don't expect this to be easy. And I don't want to leave until I've all the answers Matthew can give.'

He put a hand on her arm. 'I'll do it if you like.'

She climbed out. 'No,' she said. 'I'll do it myself. But thanks anyway.'

He gave her a thumbs-up sign. 'Why here, though, Joanna?'

She glanced around at the rural domesticity. 'I'm hoping by coming here,' she said, 'to shock him into telling me the whole story at last.'

The house was approached by a narrow path of stone flags. Joanna pushed open the wicket gate and walked up to the door.

It took courage to drop the knocker down hard enough to make a noise. Her first attempt bounced – soundlessly on the wood. The second clanged loudly enough to wake the dead.

Jane Levin opened the door. They had not met since the night at the restaurant but Joanna had never forgotten the ice-cold stare of those blue eyes and the pale, Scandinavian beauty of her blonde hair. Nor the tight line of her thin lips. She stared at Joanna.

'You,' she said.

'Detective Inspector Piercy,' Joanna said, cursing the quaver in her voice. She cleared her throat. 'I'd like to talk to Dr Levin.'

Jane Levin looked down her narrow nose. 'Couldn't you contact him at the hospital?' she said haughtily.

'I'm sorry. I have to talk to him now. It's about the murder of Marilyn Smith.'

'The nurse?' Her voice was sharp.

'Yes.'

The door was slammed in her face and Joanna stood on the doorstep, conscious of Mike's eyes boring holes into her. She turned and nodded at him, then the door was flung open.

'Joanna . . .' Matthew hissed. 'What the hell . . .?' He was furious.

'I need a statement from you, Dr Levin,' she said formally. 'Would you mind if I came inside?'

He glared at her. 'Why have you come here?'

'Because I couldn't waste any more time,' she said angrily. 'I'm fed up with half-truths. All along, Matthew,' she said, 'you've fed me little bits of the truth. I want it all now.'

'Are you here officially?' He glanced over her shoulder at Mike in the squad car. 'Because if you are maybe you'd better invite Tarzan in too.'

'Not quite officially,' she said. 'And that's a favour to you ... Matthew,' she said softly. 'This is a murder case.'

He stared at her dumbly, suddenly appalled at her manner. 'Joanna,' he begged. 'Not here. Darling, not here.' A shadow crossed his face. 'If you come inside ...' He took a deep breath. 'It will violate my home.'

'Then the station,' she said, 'and a formal, taped interview. And you're bloody lucky to get the choice. This case has its own violations, Matthew.'

'All right, Joanna,' he said. 'You win.' He turned round and she followed him into the house.

There was no sign of his wife as he led Joanna along a dark corridor lined with macs and wellies and an old bike. Matthew brushed against it as he passed and it wobbled and almost fell. He gave a quiet curse and steadied it. His hand was shaking. At the end of the corridor he opened a panelled door into a light, square study, lined with books from ceiling to floor, with two long windows facing out towards the crags in the distance and armchairs either side of the fireplace. He sat in one of them and motioned her to the other.

She tried not to look at the shelf of photographs, the centre one especially ... Matthew and Jane, bride and groom. And she wondered how many evenings they had sat in these chairs and talked, read, listened to music together.

Matthew leaned forward, biting his lip. 'You don't belong here,' he said.

'Well, I don't exactly feel comfortable either,' she bit back. 'So you'd better unload yourself and then I needn't return. I can leave you both alone.'

He looked serious. 'Will it all have to come out? Will it mean prosecutions?'

She shrugged. 'I don't know,' she said. 'It depends on the circumstances.' She leaned forward. 'Matthew, your best chance is to be frank. Please – tell me absolutely everything. As far as I can I'll help you. I promise.'

He nodded, settled back in his chair, closed his eyes. 'Thank God for someone I can trust,' he said. Then, 'Actually, you know a lot of it.'

She grimaced. 'I think I know about all of it,' she said. 'Except the most important parts.'

He ignored her comment. 'Jonah, Paul and I were in medical school together.' He paused. 'Paul always had peculiar tendencies.' He stopped. 'You know the rest of that bit. So then there was Jonah and me. We muddled along, got drunk, did our studies, sat exams together. And then he met Pamella . . .' He smiled. 'Fell for her, hook, line and sinker.' He stopped again. 'Pamella was really lovely,' he said. 'Sexy and beautiful and very clever. And Marilyn was her great friend. Plump and plain. But she was clever too, in a devious way. She'd hang around Pamella and pick up all the discarded boyfriends – came to think of them as her right. Until Jonah. Pamella didn't give him up and I think Marilyn just waited. Anyway,' he carried on, 'Pamella and Jonah got married. I was best man, Marilyn their bridesmaid. And Jonah came into general practice here in Leek. Then Pamella got pregnant.' He paused and rubbed his forehead with the palm of his hand.

'Right from the start we all knew something was terribly wrong. Even in the early weeks she was very strange.' He looked at Joanna. 'Do you know what the phrase puerperal psychosis means?'

'A sort of madness,' she ventured, 'connected with having a baby?'

He nodded and smiled. A glimpse of the old Matthew returned. 'So you do listen when I lecture you! Anyway, when the baby was born she got quite a lot worse.'

'Stevie,' she said, beginning to understand.

Matthew's face crumpled. 'Oh, God,' he said. 'You have no idea. He was so sweet . . . plump and pink and always chuckling. They called him Stevie after Pamella's father. He had been a surgeon in Manchester – a very clever man. He died a month before Stevie was born.'

'Go on. What happened?'

'After Stevie was born,' Matthew said, 'Jonah hardly dared leave her. He was so worried about what would happen.' He paused. 'I think we all had the most appalling sense of dread. We knew something was going to happen. We could feel it getting nearer. But there wasn't anything any of us could do to prevent it. Jonah tried. He stayed at home for as long as he could but financially he had to return to work or lose his practice. And all the time we were all terrified to leave them alone together.'

'Couldn't she have gone to hospital?'

'She had a short stay but got much worse. They wanted to separate mother and son and she got hysterical and threatened to kill herself. Jonah felt she might get better if she could remain at home. We all thought it was the only chance she had – if we treated her as a normal mum we thought she might snap out of it.'

'God, Matthew,' Joanna said. 'You're a doctor. Had you no judgement?'

Matthew looked away. 'It's easy with hindsight,' he said bitterly. 'Bloody easy after the event. We took turns in going round and checking on her. Things did seem to get a bit better.' He stopped. 'I suppose we all relaxed.

'Then one day Jonah came home a bit late from work. Pamella was sitting on the stairs. He told us afterwards it was very quiet in the house. Pamella told him Stevie was asleep.' Matthew closed his eyes. 'Pamella said not to worry, Stevie wouldn't cry again. Joanna . . .' Matthew's eyes were bright with unshed tears. 'He was dead in his cot. There wasn't a mark on him. He just looked asleep.

181

We hoped it was a cot death. But underneath we were so afraid.' He waited and watched Joanna carefully and she knew there was more.

'I had to do the post-mortem... This little child I'd rocked to sleep for most of his short life, Jo,' he said brokenly. 'There were cotton fibres in his lungs.'

She frowned. 'I'm sorry,' she said. 'I don't understand.'

Matthew gave a tight smile. 'You don't know everything yet, then, Detective Inspector,' he said. 'Stevie had been smothered. He had inhaled cotton fibres from a pillow. And there were other findings too. When I went to Jonah's house later that night I saw a pillow on the spare bed. It was dented. And when I looked at the cot the blankets were all over the place.' He dropped his head down into his hands. 'He must have struggled,' he said.

Joanna felt her face grow stiff with shock. The picture was the ugliest of all the pictures this case had brought to mind. The baby struggling... The expression of the mother pressing the pillow into the baby's face until it fell quiet.

The room was silent.

And now she understood. 'You certified it as a cot death,' she said, 'when Pamella Wilson belonged in Broadmoor. She was criminally insane.'

Matthew shook his head. 'She was disturbed,' he said, 'but it was to do with having a baby. No more pregnancies and she would be fine. There was no danger to any one else. It was not the psychology of a murderer.'

She clenched her fists. 'Oh, really, Matthew?' she said. 'I think you should think again. It was another error of judgement, wasn't it?'

He bowed his head.

And now she was merciless. 'It was a huge bloody cover-up! The whole damned medical profession ganged up together. She murdered her baby!' She was silent for a moment, then her anger erupted. 'How bloody convenient to have you as a friend, Matthew. It must be great having a pathologist as a pal when your wife's just murdered your baby.'

Matthew winced. 'It wasn't like that,' he protested. 'The trial . . . the court case . . . the interrogation . . .'

'By some heavy-footed police person like me,' she demanded, 'who happens to believe murder is wrong? Damn it, Mat,' she said, 'the law can be sensitive too, you know. She would simply have received psychiatric treatment.'

'And where would that have left the family doctor? Who would have gone to him with their problems? It would have finished Jonah.'

'He could have moved,' she said. 'He could have practised elsewhere.'

Matthew stared beyond her, out of the window to the grey crags in the distance. 'Yes,' he said.

'So where did Marilyn fit into all this?'

'Jonah advertised for a nurse to help him with the work,' Matthew said reluctantly. 'She answered and Jonah thought an old friend might be good for Pamella.'

'Instead of which she blackmailed Jonah . . .' Joanna finished. 'And, I suppose, tried to pick up her friend's husband. So how did she find out about the baby?'

'I'd kept a copy of the old original post-mortem report,' Matthew said slowly. 'Jonah and I agreed that it might be necessary. It was in the safe with sensitive information. Marilyn had access to the safe for staff notes, drugs information. We never thought she'd snoop . . . you trust a nurse.'

He stopped. 'I know what else was in there,' he said. 'The psychiatrist's report on Paul Haddon. He was assessed following some treatment . . .' He looked at Joanna.

'And then she started blackmailing,' Joanna said. 'I suppose she got money out of a lot of other people as well as Jonah.'

'He increased her salary,' he said. 'But what she really wanted was for him to divorce Pamella, put her away somewhere in an institution and marry her. She fancied being the doctor's wife.' Matthew stared hard at Joanna. 'You understand what I'm saying,' he said. 'It was the status she wanted.' He paused. 'She kept having all those bloody operations – breast implants, liposuction, teeth crowned in porcelain. What she didn't realize was that everything she did made Jonah more repulsed.'

'So he killed her.'

The door burst open and a small girl in jodhpurs and a yellow sweater ran in and threw her arms around Matthew. 'Daddy, Daddy, Daddy . . . you said you'd watch me jump Sparky before tea. I've gone over four times and I didn't fall off once.' She tugged at his hand. 'Come on,' she said. 'Come on.'

Matthew looked fondly down at his wife's clone. 'In a minute, Eloise,' he said, stroking the girl's pale plait. 'In a minute.'

Joanna stood up. 'I'll see myself out,' she said.

Mike was sitting far down in the seat, his feet propped up on the dashboard. He struggled to sit up as she opened the door. 'Get what you want, Joanna?'

She slammed the door. 'Yes and no,' she said.

But she was hauling them in, kicking and struggling: Paul Haddon, Grenville Machin . . . Jonah, Matthew, and the pathetic Pamella. They could fight as hard as they liked but it was futile. They were caught and she would spill them out into the legal system, one by one.

# Chapter 17

The forensic report on the coat dug up in Evelyn Shiers' garden was sitting on her desk the following morning. The coat had been buried for around five years and held no blood, no skin, but there were some white hairs. Jock Shiers had been renowned for having a full head of jet black hair.

Joanna sat, puzzled, disappointed that there was so little to be gleaned from what had seemed so promising. She glanced again at the report. It stressed that no one had met a bloody end while wearing the coat. So why bury it? And where was Jock Shiers? She sighed, pushed the report aside and looked at Mike.

'I want to talk to the woman Jonah Wilson visited the night of the murder.'

Mike looked puzzled. 'We've already been there once.'

'I know . . .' Joanna was fumbling with the truth. 'I just don't think we asked the right questions. We checked up that he'd been. I want exact times. I want to know how long he was out for. How long it would have taken him to get there. How long he spent in the house.'

'OK.' Mike stood up.

They drove to the end of the road where Jonah Wilson lived and Joanna set her watch. 'Drive slowly,' she said to Mike. 'I think he would be a cautious driver. I'll allow two minutes for him to unlock the car door, get in and drive off . . .'

Twenty minutes later they stopped outside the farmhouse door, after a long, slow drive over narrow moorland roads with tight bends and steep hills. The farm was at the end of a long, gated drive.

Fay Dunwood looked unhappily at them. 'He did come here,' she insisted. 'Dr Wilson did come ... I did have a headache. He gave me an injection and waited for it to work.'

'How long was he here for?'

'I don't know.' She was impatient with the police, protective of her doctor. 'All I know is I was worried. I'd rung earlier on in the day. Mrs Wilson said there was a lot of meningitis around. She said to ring back at eleven o'clock. The headache got worse ... Ask my husband there.'

Joanna looked at Mike. 'And he came straight out?'

The man in the corner grunted. 'He must have done. I did ring again but after that there was no answer. I thought I'd better give him instructions ... This place isn't easy to find. He could have got lost. But he was already on his way. Got here a quarter of an hour later. I was going to tell him I'd meet him at the bottom with a torch. Open them gates for him. But he weren't in.'

'And his wife?' Joanna struggled to sound casual.

'She weren't in neither – unless she'd gone to bed.'

'So, he went on the visit.' Joanna looked at Mike. 'And she must have left the house.'

'But everyone says she never goes out.'

'Does that give her an alibi?' She paused. 'What do you think, Mike? She wasn't there. Mr Dunwood rang the house and she wasn't there. I think she was in the house in Silk Street murdering her old friend who she feared was going to rob her of her husband or expose the murder of her child.'

Mike shook his head. 'Joanna,' he said. 'It won't work. How did she get past the dog? And how could she possibly have known that her husband would get called out, be gone for an hour?'

Her face dropped. 'That's the only bit I haven't worked out yet, Mike.' She grinned. 'Give me time.'

They pulled up outside Jonah Wilson's house and she sat and looked at the modest, run-down semi. 'Marilyn Smith must have milked them of an awful lot of money,' she said. She walked up the path and saw Pamella peering through the frosted glass in the front door.

'Can I come in?' Joanna called out. 'It's the police.' She held up her card, knowing Pamella would not be able to read it.

Pamella opened the door and peeped round like a shy child. 'Hello,' she said. 'I remember you.'

'Is the doctor in?'

'Jonah's at work.' Pamella smiled self-consciously. 'He works very hard, you know.'

'Yes, I do know.'

'Do you want to wait for him? You can sit with me.'

'Thank you.'

Joanna sat opposite Pamella Wilson and watched her fiddle with the material of her skirt. Then Pamella looked up and smiled. 'She is dead, isn't she?'

Joanna nodded and Pamella curled her ankles around the legs of the chair. 'Did you know,' she asked pleasantly, 'we used to be friends? Quite good friends.' She paused. 'Best friends.'

Joanna smiled back. 'Really?' she said. 'Would you like to tell me about it?'

Pamella put her head on one side, considering, then she gave an abrupt laugh. 'I suppose I could, couldn't I?' She stopped. 'Well,' she said. 'We were student nurses together. Washed the bedpans in the same machine.'

Joanna nodded. 'Why did you kill her, Pamella?' she asked.

Pamella looked surprised. 'I didn't think anyone knew,' she said thoughtfully, then she turned her clear gaze on Joanna. 'How did you know?' she asked.

'It's my job,' Joanna said.

Pamella seemed to accept this. 'Well, if you know already,' she said, almost crossly, 'what's the point of me telling you?'

'I don't know it all.'

Pamella looked pleased. 'Don't you?' She looked across the room, abstracted and vague, and Joanna waited patiently.

'Marilyn found it useful to be my friend,' Pamella said after a long silence. 'You see, when I finished with a boyfriend they used to go out with her instead, for a while.' She stopped. 'They thought they could stay near me that way.' Joanna would have accused anyone else but this sad figure of conceit. But Pamella was obviously not conceited.

'I didn't let her have Jonah.' Pamella paused as though to think why. 'He was too precious,' she said. 'You see, I loved him myself. And he loved me, you know.' There was another long pause. 'But she wanted him too.'

Joanna hardly dared breathe. She wanted this answer so much . . .

'I think . . . I think things would have been all right but I fell ill,' Pamella said quietly. 'You see I had a baby – a little boy. And he made me ill.' She looked at Joanna. 'I did love him but he made me ill. He was naughty. He used to cry.'

She leaned forward and touched Joanna's knee with a surprisingly soft, gentle stroke. 'His name was Stevie. He made me ill and I couldn't work any more. I couldn't have any old nurse working for Jonah.' She peered at Joanna with a conspiratorial air. 'She might have been pretty, like I once was. She might have tempted him.' The last few words were spoken in a whisper, Pamella Wilson peering around the room for listeners.

'So I asked my old friend. My old, ugly friend. I asked her to do my work for me.' She licked her lips. 'The trouble was, she wasn't my friend. Not at all.' Pamella's breath quickened. 'First of all she wanted money from us. She knew about Stevie being so naughty and she knew I had to punish him.' Tears started to run down Pamella's face. She made no attempt to mop them up but let them drip from her chin on to the old, black sweater.

'Jonah didn't mind. He forgave me. He understood. But she didn't. She just wanted money.' Pamella leaned forwards. 'She was a greedy, greedy woman. And she spent all the money trying to make herself beautiful.' She paused. 'I was worried,' she said. 'I thought one day the surgeon's knife would succeed where nature had failed. I thought one day she would come back beautiful. She had a lot of money, you know. At first she was foul and ugly. But she wanted Jonah.'

She paused and her face clouded over. 'I . . . I wasn't worried – at first. Jonah loved me . . . Then one day she rang me up and told me he had kissed her.'

She slowly unwound her ankles from the chair leg. 'I couldn't manage without Jonah,' Pamella said in a matter-of-fact voice. 'I had to be careful. And I had to be clever but I did have to kill her.' She held her hands out to Joanna. 'You do understand – don't you?'

Joanna nodded.

'Jonah watches me, you know. I don't have a lot of time on my own. He's very careful. I know he worries about me.'

'What did you do?'

'I planned,' Pamella said. 'I planned very carefully. And I wrote her a letter.' She smiled. 'I wrote it in Jonah's handwriting. I'm quite good at that,' she added. 'I pretended that he'd slip out when he was on call, pretended that silly Pamella would not be suspicious. I put a capsule in the letter – told her it was a special aphrodisiac.' She smiled. 'Marilyn believed anything, you know, especially things she didn't know about – things like love and sex . . .'

'What was really in the capsule?'

'Oh, some medication,' Pamella said coolly. 'Phenobarbitone. Remember, Inspector. I used to be a nurse. I know how much to give. The same as the insulin. I knew without reading that article.'

'Where did the insulin come from?'

189

Pamella opened her eyes very wide. 'Jonah's bag, of course,' she said.

Then Joanna asked the all-important question. 'How could you have known that Jonah would go out that night – and for such a long time? How could you be sure you'd be left alone?'

Pamella looked pleased with herself. 'I tell you, Inspector,' she said. 'I can be very clever . . . very clever.' She waited for the words to sink in, then asked, 'You'd like to know that, wouldn't you?' She stopped and thought for a moment. 'I bet you can't work it out, can you?'

'No.' Joanna was forced to admit it. The call to the farm had seemed genuine. There was no question of complicity. How could Pamella have known Jonah would leave her for more than half an hour?

'You know,' she said, 'in some ways that was the cleverest bit of all. I'll tell you.' She smiled. 'I did have a bit of luck. You see, I asked Marilyn, in the letter, to ring him herself half an hour after she had swallowed the capsule. She was to pretend to be a patient in one of the farthest farms away . . . a man with a weak heart. And she was to say she was his neighbour and he had chest pain – again.' Pamella stopped. 'Marilyn had a very deep voice,' she said. 'Did you know that?'

Joanna shook her head. 'No,' she said. 'No one told me.'

'Jonah is a conscientious doctor,' Pamella said. 'I knew he would have gone straight away. I would have an hour.' She smiled. 'It only took fifteen minutes,' she said. 'And wasn't I lucky? Marilyn didn't need to make that call at all. Mrs Dunwood did it for me.' She smiled again. 'And she didn't even know she was helping me. Isn't that nice?

'So I walked quickly round to Marilyn's house.' A shadow crossed her face. 'So grand,' she said disdainfully. 'So ostentatious, isn't it? Didn't you think it was, Inspector?'

Joanna nodded. 'But what about Ben? How did you get past him?'

'I had Ben as a puppy,' Pamella said. 'I gave him to

Marilyn when Stevie was born. It was a present. Didn't you know that either? He knew me. He welcomed me, licked me all over and when I told him to sit in his basket he did.'

It was the final clincher.

Now Joanna had a full case but Pamella wanted to share the details. 'It was really easy, you know, Inspector,' she said. 'You have no idea how very easy it was. If you know just a few things about how people's bodies work, to kill is extremely easy. She died quite quickly. Not like Stevie.' She licked her lips. 'He was naughty. He struggled, quite a lot.' She smiled. 'If more people knew how easy killing was perhaps more people would do it.' She started giggling. 'Like sex. You see it's quite quick. One minute there's a person struggling inside a body. The next minute there's just a body. And there's no one there. However hard you shout they don't answer.' She stopped. 'Funny, isn't it?'

Joanna felt sick.

'I could probably kill lots of people, if I wanted to. But I don't. I just hated her. That's why I killed her. I hated her.'

The thought flashed through Joanna's mind that this was how Jane Levin hated her. Pure, concentrated hatred. Hatred that could kill. The thought was overwhelming. And listening to Pamella Wilson's story was like having a knife turning in her stomach.

'She was lying there all dopey wearing such silly clothes.' Pamella started to laugh a dry, cracking laugh. 'Like the harlots of Babylon. Jonah couldn't have made love to her looking like that even if he had liked her in the first place.' Her eyes looked blue and clear. 'And he didn't like her, Inspector. I am sure now that he didn't like her. I've thought about it and I think I was mistaken. I don't think he liked her – not one little bit.'

'But she liked him?'

'They told me so at the surgery,' Pamella said. 'Maureen came round here one day.' She stopped. 'Sally and

191

Maureen are so loyal, Inspector. I know they were on my side. Maureen held my hand and told me I must try to get better. The doctor was being subjected to temptation. I asked her to keep me informed. And she did.'

'May I ask you something else, Mrs Wilson?' Joanna said.

Pamella smiled politely. 'Certainly.'

'They told me you never went out. How did you walk to Silk Street?'

'I never went out,' Pamella said, 'because I never wanted to. It isn't that I'm frightened. You see – here I'm near Stevie. But that night I left him because I had a mission,' she said grandly. 'A job to do.'

She started picking again at her skirt. 'She was wrong,' she said. 'Evil. She took money off Jonah.' Her eyes bored into Joanna's. 'You see,' she whispered, looking back over her shoulder before she spoke, 'she knew about Stevie. She knew. She found out. I don't know how she found out. I thought she was my friend. But she wasn't. You see,' she said simply, 'the trouble is, you think you can trust a nurse. But sometimes you can't.'

There was a terrible poignancy about the words. Pamella Wilson too had been a nurse.

'What did you do with the syringe?'

Pamella looked at her as though she was stupid. 'I put it in the sharps box,' she said. 'It's full of syringes. One more wasn't going to be noticed. Where better to hide one?'

'And the letter?'

'It was on the table. I picked it up.'

Then again without warning tears started rolling down her cheeks. 'I want my little boy back,' she said. 'I want Stevie ... Sometimes now I think he didn't mean to be naughty ...'

Joanna left Pamella Wilson in the custody of two policewomen and returned to Mike in the car.

'Is she crazy?' he asked.

She wound back the tape recorder and switched it on. 'If you know just a few things about how people's bodies work, to kill is extremely easy.' Pamella's voice was calm. 'One minute there's a person struggling inside a body. The next minute there's just a body . . .' She turned the tape recorder off and looked at Mike.

'I hope so,' she said with feeling. 'Because if that's sane . . .' She sighed. 'We'll let the experts work out her mental state. Thank God that isn't part of my job.'

# Chapter 18

The Super was happy. Jowls vibrating, eyebrows meeting in the middle, he grinned. He offered Joanna a glass of sherry and she accepted.

'Sit down, Piercy,' he said enthusiastically. 'Sit down. You've earned a rest. Well done.' He handed her a thimbleful of pale sherry. 'Well done. I'm glad to have it wrapped up so neatly.'

She sipped the sherry and wondered. How he could call it neatly . . .?

'She won't go to prison,' he said cheerfully. 'Not like Machin . . . Now he was a crook.' His eyes looked merry. 'There's a difference, Piercy.'

'Yes, sir.'

He walked round to the front of the desk and startled her by slapping her hard on the shoulder. 'I think we can safely say you've justified our belief in you, Piercy.'

She finished her sherry. 'Thank you, sir.'

'Greater things . . .' he said cryptically.

'I'm happy where I am,' she said. 'I like doing the job, not writing about it.'

'We're watching you,' he said, and it felt more of a threat than a promise. Big Brother . . .

He stared at her. 'Just watch your personal life, Piercy.' He stopped. 'You know what I mean.'

'Yes, sir.'

'So on with the paperwork,' he said, back to the comradeship.

*

194

She took a detour on the way home and passed Marilyn Smith's house in Silk Street. Vivian Smith hadn't wasted much time. The For Sale sign was firmly stuck in the front garden. And there was no sign of the red car.

On impulse she stopped and walked up the path to the bungalow.

Evelyn Shiers opened the door. 'They got the person, then,' she said.

Joanna nodded. 'I came to talk to you,' she said. 'I came to warn you. We won't give up on your husband. He'll remain on our files until you tell me where he is. You do know, don't you?'

Evelyn scratched her chin. 'I don't see it's any of your business,' she said. 'He's my husband. If I don't report him missing what business is it of yours?'

'It's our business,' Joanna assured her. 'And you know what a nuisance we can be. Be reasonable. Why don't you tell me?' she urged. 'What was Marilyn blackmailing you about? Whose was the coat?'

Evelyn seemed to crumple at mention of the coat. 'If Jock found out,' she said. 'If he found out, Inspector, I think he'd kill me.'

'He probably won't need to find out.'

She looked sulky. 'I won't have him back,' she said.

'Nobody expects you to.' Joanna was getting exasperated. She wanted to get home to a long soak in the bath. She was tired, and flat, in the way that she always was after an intensive and exhausting case. She wanted to wind it up, finish the paperwork – and forget it.

'He took off on his boat,' Evelyn said. 'Told me he wanted to go round the world. That was four years ago. Left me no money.' Her eyes opened wide. 'He wanted me to go with him.'

Joanna smothered a giggle. The picture of Evelyn Shiers a round-the-world yachtswoman, tied to a ship's wheel, was too much after all the ugly visual conjurings of the last week or so. She laughed out loud and watched the bristling fox look offended. 'I'm sorry.' She quickly apologized, then added, 'So whose was the coat?'

Evelyn looked down at the floor. 'I was lonely,' she said. 'I went to the pub one night.' She looked up. 'No harm in that,' she said. 'I'm not used to drinking. He brought me home. Left his coat. I didn't know his name. Marilyn must have seen. I was worried Jock might come home and find it. And she was threatening to say all sorts of things.' Her eyes were bloodshot. 'Jock is a jealous man,' she said. 'He would have believed her – all the lies. He would have swallowed them all. I didn't know what to do,' she said. 'There was no one . . . no one I could talk to. So I buried the coat.'

Joanna sighed. How often had she heard that same phrase, 'There was no one I could talk to.'

'Would you like us to try and find Jock?'

Evelyn pressed her lips together and gave a sudden confused look. 'I don't know, Inspector,' she said. 'I really don't know. It's been a very long time.'

Joanna lay in the bath, luxuriating in scented oils, listening to the answerphone switch itself on . . . She heard Matthew's voice. 'Jo . . .' then silence, and peace.

She stayed in the bath until the water grew cold.

# ALLISON & BUSBY CRIME

**Jo Bannister**
A Bleeding of Innocents
Sins of the Heart
Burning Desires

**Simon Beckett**
Fine Lines
Animals

**Denise Danks**
Frame Grabber
Wink a Hopeful Eye
The Pizza House Crash

**John Dunning**
Booked to Die

**Bob George**
Main Bitch

**Russell James**
Slaughter Music

**H. R. F. Keating**
A Remarkable Case of
  Burglary

**Ted Lewis**
Billy Rags
Get Carter
GBH
Jack Carter's Law
Jack Carter and the
  Mafia Pigeon

**Ross Macdonald**
Blue City
The Barbarous Coast
The Blue Hammer
The Far Side of the Dollar
Find a Victim
The Galton Case
The Goodbye Look
The Instant Enemy
The Ivory Grin
The Lew Archer Omnibus
  Vol 1

The Lew Archer Omnibus
  Vol 2
Meet Me at the Morgue
The Moving Target
Sleeping Beauty
The Underground Man
The Way Some People Die
The Wycherly Woman
The Zebra-Striped Hearse

**Margaret Millar**
Ask for Me Tomorrow
Mermaid
Rose's Last Summer
Banshee
How Like An Angel
The Murder of Miranda
A Stranger in My Grave
The Soft Talkers

**Sax Rohmer**
The Fu Manchu Omnibus
  Volume I
The Fu Manchu Omnibus
  Volume II

**Richard Stark**
The Green Eagle Score
The Handle
Point Blank
The Rare Coin Score
Slayground
The Sour Lemon Score
The Parker Omnibus
  Volume 1

**Donald Thomas**
Dancing in the Dark

**I. K. Watson**
Manor
Wolves Aren't White

**Donald Westlake**
Sacred Monsters
The Mercenaries
The Donald Westlake Omnibus